I'd never met anyone like him before. . . .

When I spotted Peter, my heart rate doubled. *What if he doesn't remember me?* I thought as I rolled down the window.

He remembered me. "Fill 'er up, Sleeping Beauty?" he asked, giving me a slow smile.

"Yes. Thanks," I said somewhat breathlessly.

Peter filled up the tank—I only needed three gallons—and I paid him. I hesitated with my right hand on the key in the ignition. I couldn't just drive away. I wanted something to happen. My tongue was tied in a knot, though. *How do you make the first move?* I wondered, wishing for the first time in my life that I knew how to flirt.

As it turned out, I didn't need to make the first move. Opening the door on the other side of my car, Peter climbed into the passenger seat. "I'm off work as of now," he told me. "Want to go to a party?"

"It's a school night," I pointed out.

He grinned. "So?"

"So . . ." I thought about all the homework I still had to do. I thought about Mom waiting for me at home. Mom . . . and Hal. "So nothing," I said. "Let's go."

Don't miss any books in this dramatic new series:

THE YEAR
I TURNED
Sixteen

Available from ARCHWAY Paperbacks

THE YEAR I TURNED
Sixteen

DAISY

Diane Schwemm

AN ARCHWAY PAPERBACK
Published by POCKET BOOKS
New York   London   Toronto   Sydney   Tokyo   Singapore

AN ARCHWAY PAPERBACK *Original*

An Archway Paperback published by
POCKET BOOKS, a division of Simon & Schuster Inc.
1230 Avenue of the Americas, New York, NY 10020

Produced by Seventeenth Street Productions, Inc.,
a division of Daniel Weiss Associates, Inc.

ISBN: 0-671-00441-7

First Archway Paperback printing September 1998

10 9 8 7 6 5 4 3 2 1

AN ARCHWAY PAPERBACK and colophon are
registered trademarks of Simon & Schuster Inc.

Printed in the U.S.A.

IL 7+

For Josh and Evan

One

Catch this one, Daze!"

My older sister, Rose, pulled back her arm and tossed the Frisbee as far as she could. The bright orange disk sailed in my direction . . . sort of. Sprinting across the sand, I splashed into the water and jumped into the air, snagging the Frisbee before it could slice into the waves. Back on the beach Rose and her boyfriend, Stephen Mathias, clapped and whistled. "Nice catch!" Stephen yelled. I grinned at them and took a deep bow.

Just then my mother called out, "Food's ready." I lobbed the Frisbee to Stephen and jogged over to join my family. It was a warm August evening, and we were having a clambake at Kettle Cove, a little beach on the edge of town, to celebrate my sixteenth birthday. Balloons were tied to the picnic table, and lobsters, steamers, and ears of sweet corn had been roasting over a fire in a pit in the sand. Living in Maine is the best.

We started with paper plates piled high with steamers. I watched Rose take a ton of them. She has long blond hair and blue eyes, and she looked incredibly pretty in a lace-trimmed tank top and

1

gauzy flowered skirt. No one looks glamorous eating steamers, though. "Yum," she said, dipping a clam in melted butter and then popping it into her mouth.

My mom, Maggie Walker, tossed the salad while her friend Hal Leverett, our neighbor, filled plastic glasses with lemonade. Mom has short blond hair that she pushes behind her ears—she's forty now, and she's still the most beautiful woman I know.

We were all gobbling steamers—Mom too. Stephen watched my family eat, his arms folded across his chest, his own plate empty. "I still haven't gotten over the way you natives put away clams," he admitted, his brown eyes twinkling. "By the *pound.* And I bet you'll devour a couple of lobsters apiece when you're finished."

Rose laughed. "It's a Maine thing. You wouldn't understand."

Stephen turned to my twelve-year-old sister, Laurel, whose gold-streaked brown hair was pulled back in a ponytail. She had a lobster bib on over her usual grass-stained overalls. "How do *you* do it, Toad?" Stephen asked, using the nickname Rose gave Laurel a few years ago. "Clams and lobsters are your friends."

Laurel considered this question thoughtfully as she wiped some butter off her lips with a paper napkin. She's the animal lover in the family, but when it comes to clambakes, she's as carnivorous as the rest of us. "It's a food chain thing," she explained to Stephen, "and we're at the top."

"Right," I said. "Eating shellfish is our destiny."

Mom passed out claw crackers for the lobsters. "They eat seafood in Boston, too," she pointed out to Stephen, whose family moved up to Maine when he started high school at nearby Seagate Academy.

"In restaurants, mostly," replied Stephen. "I never met a lobster in person before it ended up in a pot."

Rose rested her head on Stephen's shoulder, her blondness a contrast to his dark brown hair. "Aren't we uncivilized?" she said happily.

My youngest sister, ten-year-old Lily, was buttering a hot ear of corn. "This is the best, Mom," she said. "I'm going to eat until I burst."

"Everything's great," I agreed. "Thanks, Mom."

"A clambake cooks itself," she said, brushing aside our praise with typical modesty.

"Hey, we almost forgot to toast the birthday girl." Rose raised her glass. "I can't believe you're sixteen, Daisy. That means I'm *really* old!"

Rose graduated from South Regional High School last June—she's eighteen. "Right, you're ancient," I kidded.

"No, but seriously," said Rose. "It seems like just yesterday *I* was turning sixteen." A shadow crossed her face, dimming her hundred-watt smile for a second. Rose's sixteenth birthday hadn't been such a happy occasion. Our father had died in a boating accident just a few months before the birthday. We were all silent for a moment, thinking the same thoughts, I guess. Then Rose's face brightened again. "Remember back when Daisy liked baseball better than boys?"

Everybody laughed. I rolled my eyes. Just a few days ago my first boyfriend, Jay McGuigan, and I had broken up. I'd gone down to Boston for a Red Sox doubleheader with Tommy Bradford, this guy in my class whose dad coaches at the high school, and it was absolutely *not* a date, but Jay got absurdly jealous and we had a huge fight and that was that. "Last week I liked boys better," I told Rose with a grin. "This week I'm back to baseball."

"Let's all tell one thing we like about Daisy," Lily piped up suddenly, waving a lobster claw for attention.

"Oh, please," I groaned.

"That's a nice idea," Mom said, smiling at Lily. "You want to start?"

Lily nodded, her short blond hair bouncing. By the way, I should note here that my youngest sister was wearing a satin, twenties-era flapper dress topped off with a feather boa. To a beach party. That's Lily in a nutshell. "What *I* like about Daisy," Lily informed the group, "is that she hardly ever gets mad at me even when I really bug her."

"Except that time you lost my autographed Jim Rice baseball mitt," I reminded her.

"I said *hardly* ever," Lily said.

"I like Daisy because she's always in a sunny mood," Rose contributed. "Of course, that's also what I *don't* like about her because whenever I'm trying to enjoy a good sulk, Daisy always talks me out of it. How about you, Mom?"

Mom shook her head, smiling. "How can I pick just one thing?"

"You have to," Lily pressed.

"Okay. I like the way Daisy picks up around the house without being asked."

"Mo-o-om!" Lily complained. "That's a boring thing to like." "Well, it's true," Mom replied, winking at me.

"My turn," said Stephen. "I like how even when she was a kid, Daisy could beat me at hoops. She taught me humility."

"How about you, Laurel?" Rose prompted.

Laurel gazed at me with shining eyes. "I like how Daisy is good at everything she tries. How she gets all A's at school and is the star of the soccer team, and how she's so pretty but she isn't at all vain. I want to be just like her," she finished softly.

"Kiss up," muttered Lily.

Laurel scowled at Lily. I reached across the picnic table and punched Laurel lightly on the arm. "Thanks, Toad," I said.

Just then Mr. Leverett cleared his throat. "Well, I—," he began.

Before he could continue, I jumped to my feet. "Anyone for more lemonade?" I asked.

As I circled the table refilling glasses my mom threw me a questioning glance, but I ignored it. Maybe I'd been rude, cutting Hal off. But what's he doing here, anyway? I asked myself.

All at once my throat tightened with unexpected tears. I'd spent the picnic trying not to think about my father, but now I couldn't help it. If Dad were still alive, Mom wouldn't be bringing Hal to family parties, I thought. I didn't care if he *was* just a friend—if any man was going to be at my birthday party, I wanted it to be Dad.

I'm not the gooey sentimental type, but I know when I'm about to burst into tears. "Be right back," I muttered, depositing the lemonade jug on the table with a thud. Turning away from the others, I strode off across the sand.

I hadn't gone ten yards when I heard a voice behind me. "Daze, wait for me."

I stopped. Rose jogged after me, her skirt fluttering and her expression worried. "Are you okay?" she asked. I shrugged wordlessly, my hands stuck deep in the pockets of my shorts. "Thinking about Dad?" Rose guessed.

I hate falling apart—I almost never cry—but my voice cracked with emotion. "He should be here today."

"I know," Rose agreed.

Side by side, we walked along the water's edge. For a few minutes neither of us spoke. I knew we were both remembering the day two and a half years ago when we learned that Dad's fishing boat had been lost in a sudden storm at sea.

"I think you miss Dad the most," Rose ventured at last. "I mean, I miss him, too, but you and he were the closest. You were his favorite."

"Dad didn't play favorites," I said, but in a way I knew what she said was true. Dad had loved us all, but I was the one who'd liked going out on the boat with him. Back on land, I'd help him mend his nets and then we'd play catch on the lawn for hours until Dad was satisfied that I could throw as far and straight as a big leaguer. I look like him, too—I have his eyes and his height and his smile.

And his upbeat attitude . . . usually. Now I struggled to get back in a positive frame of mind. "Dad would be proud of how well we're doing on our own," I said as Rose and I hit the end of the beach and turned around.

"We've gotten our lives together," Rose agreed. She laughed dryly. "Not that it wasn't an uphill fight. Remember how mad I was two summers ago when Mom made me get a job? And when we had to use food stamps for a while—that freaked me out."

But things had changed. These days Rose was acting in summer stock theater—musicals mostly, because she loves to sing. In the fall she would start classes at the local community college and continue working part-time at Cecilia's, a boutique in downtown Hawk Harbor. That was the first job Rose got, back when she was sixteen. Mom had started a catering business about a year after Dad died and she was doing well, but money was still a little tight, so we'd all found ways to pitch in this summer vacation. I baby-sat and did yard work. Laurel ran a dog wash with her friend Jack Harrison in Jack's backyard. "We're a lot more independent than we used to be," I concluded.

"You were always that way, though," Rose said. "You didn't whine like me and Laurel and Lily." She laughed again. "It used to drive me crazy!"

I shrugged. "I just felt like I had to do whatever it took to hold our family together."

We were back at the picnic table. "Just in time, Daisy Claire Walker," Mom called. "We can't cut the cake without you!"

Mom had baked a triple-layer carrot cake piled high with cream cheese frosting—my favorite. As she lit the candles everyone began singing "Happy Birthday to You." Rose snapped her fingers and threw in a bluesy harmony—she has a great voice.

"Make a wish, Daisy," Lily shouted when the song was over.

I closed my eyes. What should I wish for? A million dollars? A new car? An unbeaten season this fall with the South Regional High varsity girls' soccer team?

I want us all to be safe, I wished silently. Just the way we are right now. No more changes.

I opened my eyes again, and as my sisters cheered I blew out all sixteen candles on my cake.

Hawk Harbor is a small town on the coast of southern Maine. I was born there and so were all my sisters—our parents grew up here, too. When I was younger, we lived in a big Victorian house on Lighthouse Road that had been in the family for generations, but after Dad died, we had to sell it. Now we rent a two-floor apartment in an old brick building on Main Street above Wissinger's Bakery.

A week after my birthday I spent the afternoon baby-sitting. Then I stopped at our old neighbors, the

Schenkels, to mow their lawn and clip their hedges. By the end of the day I was pretty tired, so I pedaled home more slowly than usual. Going through the center of town, I waved to Mr. Appleby, who was out in front of his hardware store, putting sale tags on a display of plastic lawn furniture—his daughter, Cath, is one of Rose's best friends. Half a block farther along I hopped the bike onto the sidewalk so I could shout hello through the open door of Cecilia's to my sister, who was behind the cash register.

Reaching the bakery, I squeezed the hand brakes. Before pushing my bike into the storage room in the back of the building, though, I stood for a minute, looking toward the sea. Old fishing boats and sleek yachts motored in and out of the busy harbor, summing up my town: part blue-collar New England town, part upscale summer resort.

Mom was in the kitchen when I went in, slicing vegetables. "Something smells good," I said as I rummaged in the fridge for a snack.

Mom nodded in the direction of the industrial-size oven she'd installed when she quit her old job to cater full-time. "Appetizers for the Nickersons' anniversary party tomorrow night."

I pulled up a stool and another cutting board so I could help her chop. As I took a seat Mom looked at my necklace. "That looks nice," she said.

I put my hand to my throat. I was wearing my sixteenth-birthday present, a gold chain and an antique charm from my great-grandmother's bracelet. The charm was shaped like a seashell—Rose got one that's a rosebud for her sixteenth birthday. "A little fancy with a T-shirt and cutoffs, huh?"

She smiled. "I think it's the first jewelry I've ever seen you wear."

"I like it."

"So, how are Vera and Gil?"

I filled her in on the neighborhood gossip I'd heard from Mrs. Schenkel and told Mom that the weeds were really high in front of our old house. "Whoever bought it isn't living there."

"Probably someone planning to fix it up for a summer house," Mom speculated.

"An inn," a voice called from the living room. "The owners want to open an inn."

Hal's here again, I thought. For some reason my mood turned instantly grouchy. Lately he'd become a fixture at our dinner table. Couldn't he ever cook for himself?

"An inn," Mom mused. "Well, it's a big enough house, I suppose. And they could renovate the barn. . . ."

"So, Mom," I said, changing the subject. "I started looking for a part-time job today."

She stopped slicing mushrooms. "What?"

"Now that I'm sixteen, I want to make more money than I can from baby-sitting," I explained. "That way I could help with some of our expenses."

Mom shook her head. "You don't need to do that. And with school starting soon, you won't have time."

"But Rose got a job when *she* turned sixteen."

"Our situation was different then. You shouldn't be worrying about money, Daisy."

"I'm not worried. I just want to start saving for college, like Rose."

Mom resumed slicing, the knife blade knocking rhythmically on the wooden cutting board. "Aren't you already stretched too thin, honey? With soccer practice every day and games on weekends. You said you were thinking about running for student council, too. I'd hate to see your grades drop. You're headed for class valedictorian when you graduate."

"Just a few hours a week, Mom," I said. "I promise I'll quit if it gets to be too much."

Hal chose that moment to come into the kitchen. He had a legal pad under his arm and a pencil tucked behind his ear. He's tall and wears glasses—he's an accountant, in his late forties, who got divorced a few years ago, right before we moved in next door to him. "Couldn't help overhearing," he began in a friendly manner. "You know, my office could use some phone and filing help. It might be just what you're looking for, Daisy. If you want to come in and fill out an application, I could put in a good—"

"Thanks, anyway, but that's not really the kind of job I had in mind." I hopped down from the stool, avoiding my mom's gaze. "I'll be in my room," I said over my shoulder as I left the kitchen. "Call me if you need me, okay?"

As I went upstairs I wasn't sure why I'd responded the way I had to Hal's offer. Answering phones would be fine, and Hal is a nice enough guy. He's always been a good neighbor—he really comes through for us whenever there's a clogged drain or a disgusting bug to kill. My sisters and I are always psyched when his cute college-age sons, Kevin and Connor, visit; they're really nice. It just wasn't his business, I decided. I was talking to Mom, not him.

I wouldn't have held a grudge about it, but Hal just had to butt into every single conversation at dinner, too. I was still gritting my teeth at nine o'clock when Rose got home from her date with Stephen.

She and I share a bedroom, as do Lily and Laurel. Our room has tall, old-fashioned windows that make it seem bigger than it is. With two of everything in it—twin beds, dressers, night tables, and desks—it's pretty cramped. We've each given it our own sense of style, though. Rose has put up posters of her favorite singers and actors, and she's into incense and tapestries and flowering plants. My shelves are crowded with sports trophies, my baseball card collection, and odds and ends I saved when we moved out of our old house: some of Dad's fishing tackle, a plaque the chamber of commerce gave him one year, his toolbox.

I was sitting on my bed reading *Sports Illustrated* when Rose flopped down on her bed with a sigh. "I'm going to wither and die when Stephen leaves for Harvard," she moaned, flinging a hand to her forehead.

Rose can be pretty theatrical. "Are you doing Juliet?" I guessed. "Or Ophelia?"

"Seriously, Daze." She sat up. "It stinks."

Rose is always open with her feelings, and she'd been fretting for weeks over her upcoming separation from Stephen. He'd graduated from Seagate a year earlier, but since then he'd been in Hawk

Harbor, working as a volunteer for county social services. He wants to be a lawyer someday, the kind who represents poor people for free. "He'll come home for vacations," I said.

"But it won't be the same," Rose despaired. "I mean, we've been like *this*"—she held up her hand with the index and middle fingers crossed—"for two whole *years*." Rose quickly changed the subject. "So, Hal was over for dinner again, huh?"

"Yeah." I frowned. "What's *with* that, anyway? He's, like, *omnipresent* these days. I mean, our *other* neighbors don't come over every night."

"I sense romance blossoming," Rose said knowingly.

I blinked. "Mom? A romance with *Hal?* Are you kidding?"

"Why not?" she asked. "He and Mom have gotten to be pretty tight these past couple of years. Going out to lunch, lending each other books, that sort of thing."

"Yeah, but—"

"He has a great sense of humor for an accountant, don't you think? Nobody makes Mom laugh that hard. I think they make a cute couple."

"A *couple?*" I stared at my sister in disbelief. "You mean like . . ."

"Like who knows?" said Rose. "Maybe Mom's ready for a boyfriend. Maybe she'll even get married again someday."

I shook my head emphatically. "Mom does *not* need a boyfriend."

"Why not?"

"It's only been two and a half years since—"

"*Only* two and a half years?" Rose broke in. "What, you don't think that's long enough to grieve? Mom should join a convent or something? She deserves to have a life of her own that's not just work and kids."

I fell back on, "Yeah, but . . ."

"But *what?*" Rose said. "Don't you want Mom to be happy?"

Of course I wanted my mother to be happy—that wasn't the point. Turning my head away from Rose, I looked at the framed picture on my night table. My father smiled up at me from under the bill of a Boston Red Sox cap, his face tanned from spending his days on the water, his light blue eyes crinkled against the sun. I remembered that day as if it were yesterday. We'd all gone down to Boston, and he'd taken me to the game while Mom, Rose, Lily, and Laurel hit the aquarium and museum. Just him and me. We'd eaten three Fenway franks apiece. The Red Sox won in extra innings.

In the picture Dad looked so alive, and that was how I wanted to remember him. Am I the only person who's still loyal to you, Dad? I wondered. "But nothing," I said quietly.

Two

"Come on, girls. *Push* it!" Coach Wheeler roared.

I sprinted across the playing field, arms and legs pumping, sucking air into my lungs as deeply as I could. Out of the corner of my eye I could see Jamila Wade and Kristin McIntyre also running their hearts out. They were my teammates and my best friends, but I didn't intend to let them catch me. My muscles burned—I was going my fastest—but I made myself go faster still.

I didn't slow down until I reached the end of the field. One by one the rest of the soccer team crossed the line behind me and collapsed, panting. Hands on my hips, I walked back toward Larry Wheeler. He coaches girls' soccer *and* softball—two of my three sports—so he and I are pretty tight. He's stocky, with sun-bleached hair and light blue eyes—he reminds me a little of my dad, especially the "push it" part. It was Dad who taught me to give a hundred and ten percent to everything I do.

Which doesn't mean I don't whine sometimes. Coach Wheeler can be a slave driver. "Tell me that's the last wind sprint of the day," I begged, pushing a sweaty lock of hair off my forehead.

15

"That's it, Daiserooni." He can be goofy, too, which also reminds me of Dad. "Hey, when do you start the job?"

"Tonight," I told him.

"Good luck," he said, patting me on the shoulder. Then he shouted so everyone could hear, "Nice practice. See you tomorrow morning."

Jamila and Kristin fell into step beside me, and we headed to the South Regional High gym. When we walk in a row, Coach Wheeler says we look like a flag because we all have long hair and it's like stripes: Jamila's black braids, my bright blond ponytail, and Kristin's deep red hair. The flag was drooping a little today, though.

"Wheeler's more of a sadist than ever," Jamila observed, wiping her face on the sleeve of her T-shirt. "Double session preseason practices—does he think we're bionic or something?"

"I didn't work out all summer," Kristin admitted, rubbing her quads. "Man, I'm hurting."

I was hurting, too, but in a good way. "I like double sessions," I confessed.

Jamila shook her head. "Are you crazy?"

"She's crazy," Kristin confirmed, her green eyes twinkling. "But we knew that."

I grinned. "Come on. Doesn't it feel good afterward?"

"Maybe a *week* afterward," said Jamila, holding open the door to the gym.

"You forget Daisy thrives on pain," Kristin kidded.

"And she doesn't need sleep like the rest of us mortals," Jamila added.

Inside the girls' locker room we kicked off our cleats and stripped out of our grubby shorts and T-shirts, then hit the showers. "I'm not a masochist—I just like to win," I reminded my friends as hot water ran down my body.

"It's that simple, huh?" asked Kristin, her voice echoing in the shower stalls.

"Yep," I replied.

I thought about the conversation later, though, as I strolled into the lobby of the community hospital to start my new part-time job as a receptionist. It had been Coach Wheeler's idea—his wife, Nan, is an administrator there. I'd be working three nights a week plus Sundays, and what with school, soccer, homework, and chores at home, every minute of every day would be filled. And that's the way I like it, I realized. I don't thrive on pain, but I *do* like to be challenged. I like being tired at the end of the day, bone tired, so tired I drop right off to sleep. Too tired to think. Too tired to dream.

"It's kind of cool to be a junior," I said to some of my friends on the first day of school in September. Jamila, Kristin, and I were heading to third-period gym class. "You know, upperclassmen."

"Upperclass*women*," Jamila corrected.

"Hey, look." Kristin pointed. "They put the spring team pictures up."

We stopped to look at a row of framed photographs

on the wall outside the gym. There I was as a sophomore, with the varsity girls' softball squad. "You're all
over this wall, Walker," Jamila said to me.

I was—I play three sports, and I'd been on varsity even as a freshman. "Yeah, but so are you."
Jamila does three sports, too, although she'll probably still be JV in basketball this year.

"Daisy. I was hoping I'd run into you."

I turned around. "Hi, Mel."

Melissa Hannaway was a senior. She played softball with me, and she was president of her class last
year. "I wanted to talk to you about student council
elections," she said. "You're running, right?"

"I haven't made up my mind yet," I told her.
"I've got so much other stuff going on, you know?"

"You should run, Daze," Kristin put in. "You'd
be a great class rep."

"I'm running," Mel said. "It would be a blast if
you were on the council, too."

"I'll think about it some more," I promised.

"Just let me know so I can get your name on the
ballot," Mel said as she headed off.

"You'd be a shoo-in," Jamila said as we changed
for gym class in the locker room.

"Maybe," I said. "It *would* be fun. How many
more things can I pack into my schedule, though?"

"You can handle it," Kristin said.

"You're Supergirl," Jamila agreed.

"Super*woman*," I corrected her.

We all laughed. I *am* kind of a classic over-
achiever. But I couldn't help wondering whether

student council might be too much for me to handle. Is there such a thing as "too much"? I thought.

"That's not the way you're supposed to do it, Laurel," Lily declared. "Daisy, she's doing it wrong!"

The following Saturday my sisters and I were sitting around the kitchen table, gluing tiny pine cones and fall leaves to paper that looked like tree bark. Mom was catering a dinner party that night, and she'd given us the job of making place cards.

I inspected Laurel's handiwork. "Looks all right to me," I told Lily.

Lily pushed out her lower lip. "No, it doesn't. She's just *cramming* the leaves on instead of *arranging* them artistically."

"And I suppose you're Picasso," Laurel retorted.

They launched into one of their trademark spats. Rose looked at me. I knew she wanted me to stop them, but for once I didn't have the energy to play umpire. I'd stayed up late doing homework the night before and had gone for a five-mile run that morning.

The telephone rang. Rose practically hurdled over the table to answer it on the second ring. "Hello?" she said. "Oh, Mita, hi! How are you?"

Rose and her friend Sumita Ghosh, who had left last week for Colby College, gabbed for about fifteen minutes. While they were talking, Rose was animated, but as soon as she hung up, her expression grew gloomy. "College sounds like so much fun," she said, dropping back into her chair with a sigh. "Parties practically every night, tailgates at the football game, handsome upperclassmen . . ."

"You're going to college, too," Laurel said.

"*Community* college." Rose sniffed. "I'm still living at *home.*"

"How does Stephen like Harvard, anyway?" I asked.

Rose's gloom deepened. "He loves it," she answered, slumping down with her arms folded on the table. "The campus is beautiful, his roommates are cool, his classes are great, yada yada yada."

"Isn't that good?" I wondered.

"No. He isn't homesick at all! He's supposed to be *pining.*"

"I'm sure he misses you," I said.

"Maybe." Rose dabbed some glue onto a pine cone and stuck it haphazardly to a place card. "But face it. He was ready to get out into the real world. While I'll probably be stuck here for the rest of my life."

"At least Rox is still around," I pointed out.

Roxanne Beale, one of Rose's closest friends, was going to the community college, too. "Yeah," conceded Rose with a sigh. "Misery loves company."

"I'm done," announced Lily, pushing back her chair. "Rose, can I borrow your curling iron?"

"Sure—but what for?" Rose asked.

"To curl my hair," Lily said.

"I figured that part out. But why?"

"Because Lindsey, Talia, Kendall, and Kimberly curl *their* hair," interjected Laurel in a disdainful tone.

"Shut up, ugly" was Lily's parting shot to Laurel.

"Who are Lindsey, Talia, Kendall, and Kimberly?" I asked Laurel after Lily had flounced from the room.

"Lily's new friends from Mr. Cabot's sixth-grade class," Laurel answered. "They formed this instant clique. I see them at recess—they're like one creature with five heads."

Rose appeared as mystified as I was. "Lily's in a clique?" she said. "Isn't that one of those oxy-what-do-you-call-its?"

"Oxymorons," I supplied.

"Yeah, right," said Rose. "I mean, Lily. She's always been so . . . *different.*"

"Not anymore," said Laurel. "You should see them. They dress alike, talk alike, eat the same thing for lunch, carry the same kind of notebook, use the same shampoo."

"That's right," I said. "She wasn't wearing one of her wacky costumes just now. She was in jeans and a white T-shirt."

"New jeans," said Laurel. "Mom had to buy them for her because she wouldn't wear the old ones. They weren't the right brand."

"Sixth grade," Rose said thoughtfully. "Yeah, you know, I think that's when it starts."

"What?" I asked.

"Peer pressure."

"Speaking of which . . . ," Laurel began.

She didn't finish the sentence. "Yeah?" Rose said after a minute had passed.

"Well, do you guys remember things . . . *changing* when you got into eighth grade?"

"In what way?" Rose asked.

"Like socially. Boys."

Rose blew out a sigh of relief. "Oh, *that*."

"All of a sudden everyone's pairing up," Laurel explained. "You're not cool if you don't have a boyfriend. So yesterday in the bus line after school, Jack asked me to go out with him!"

"What did you say?" Rose asked.

"'No way,' of course." Laurel shuddered. "I mean, he's my *friend*. I don't want to be like *that* with him."

"Are you sure? Jack's pretty cute," said Rose, wiggling her eyebrows.

Laurel's face flushed hot pink. "Beyond sure. We've always been just friends. He shouldn't have pulled that on me. It made me so mad!"

I dimly remembered having the same reaction a long, long time ago when my old neighbor Kyle Cooper flirted with me. I could have commiserated with Laurel, but once again I didn't have the energy.

"Was Jack mad at you for turning him down?" Rose wanted to know.

"Maybe," said Laurel. She chewed her lip, looking worried. "Probably. Oh, I don't care!"

"Men," said Rose, clearly thinking about Stephen selfishly having fun at his new college. "Can't live with 'em, can't live without 'em. Don't you agree, Daze?"

I wasn't so sure about the "can't live without 'em" part. I hadn't missed having a boyfriend since

Jay and I broke up. But who had the energy to explain? "You bet," I said.

The next Tuesday night I got home from the hospital at ten. Lily and Laurel's room was dark; Rose was in our room, whispering on the phone to Stephen. To give her some privacy, I retreated to the kitchen for a snack. I was buttering a piece of toast when the front door to the apartment rattled open. "Is that you, Mom?" I called out.

Mom came into the kitchen. She was wearing a dress and heels. "Hi, Daisy," she said. "You're up late."

"I thought you were in bed," I told her. "Did you have a catering job tonight?"

Mom slipped off her jacket and slung it over the back of a chair. "No," she replied as she put the kettle on the stove and turned on the burner. "I went to a movie. With Hal," she added, blushing ever so slightly.

"A movie?" I repeated.

"A dumb action film," she elaborated. "There's not much choice in Kent."

Mom and Mr. Leverett had driven all the way to Kent to see a movie. This was a switch from their casual lunches and the meals he ate with us. "Was it a *date?*" I asked, choking on the word.

Mom took a tea bag from the stainless steel canister next to the stove and dropped it in a mug. "That makes it sound like we're in high school," she said, laughing a little. "But I suppose it was."

Her cheeks grew even pinker, and she smiled in

a funny way, a secretive, inward smile that somehow didn't include me. "Is that okay?" she asked, pouring hot water into her mug.

I stared down at the now cold toast. "Sure," I said, not meeting her eyes. "Uh, I'm going to hit the sack—my first soccer game's tomorrow. Good night."

"Sweet dreams, hon."

I washed up, undressed, and climbed quietly into bed so I wouldn't wake Rose, who'd fallen asleep with a picture of Stephen beside her on the pillow. I was unbelievably tired and needed a good night's rest to be in top form for my game, but for some reason I couldn't doze off. My eyes stayed open, fixed on the harvest moon shining through a gap in the curtains. It's just nerves, I decided. I was the starting varsity forward this year, and I really wanted to win our first game. That's all it is, I told myself. Nerves.

When I'm on the athletic field, I don't think about anything but the game. My eyes are everywhere at once: on the ball, on my teammates in their blue-and-gray uniforms, on my opponents, on the goal. Soccer isn't like football or baseball—it's nonstop action, and you can't afford to be distracted even for a second or you'll lose the ball, or miss a chance to pass or tackle or shoot on goal. That's why I'm good—because I can focus one hundred percent. I inherited that from Dad.

At the end of the third quarter we were tied 3–3

with the Kent High Hurricanes. Coach Wheeler called us over to the sideline for a pep talk, and as he outlined a strategy for getting around the Hurricane defense my gaze wandered to the bleachers. Mom and Lily were sitting in the front row and had been doing more than their share of shouting. Right next to Mom, also wearing a Go, Sharks! button, was . . . Mr. Leverett.

Weird—he must've taken time off from work for this, I thought. A memory came to me—uninvited and painfully fresh despite the passage of time. Dad had been at every single one of my games back in junior high.

"And pass back to Daisy," Coach Wheeler was saying, "who will have dodged number fourteen to position herself in front of the goal. Got that, Wade? Walker?"

I felt Jamila's elbow in my ribs. I'd tuned Coach Wheeler out for the first time in my life. "Sorry," I said. "Could you repeat that?"

He flashed me a funny look, then ran over the play again. I nodded briskly and the team huddled, our arms around one another and our heads close together. "Go, fight, win!" we shouted. Clapping in unison, we jogged back out on the field.

We played aggressively right off the bat, and within thirty seconds I was dribbling the ball down the field and then slicing a pass to Kristin, my arms extended for balance. A few seconds later the ball came back to me, courtesy of Jamila, and there was no one between me and the

Hurricane goalie. I nailed the net, top left-hand corner.

My teammates dashed over to congratulate me, and the home bleachers erupted in cheers. I hugged Jamila, grinning. That's all there is to it, I thought. *Go, fight, win.* If I kept that in mind and nothing else, I'd be fine.

Three

"Didn't we have pot roast a couple of days ago?" Rose asked as we set the table a week later.

She was moving clockwise, putting a napkin in front of each chair. I walked counterclockwise, laying out the silverware. "Hal's coming over for dinner, and he loves Mom's pot roast," I told Rose.

Rose smiled knowingly. "Love is in the air," she sang, and whistled the tune to some awful seventies song.

I had to admit, she seemed to be right. Hal had dropped in while Mom was making the gravy. He'd poured two glasses of red wine and was standing close to her as she cooked. I had to go in the kitchen once or twice to get the salt- and pepper shakers and salad bowls, and I couldn't help noticing how giggly they were with each other. What did Mom say the other night about dates sounding like high school? I thought. Who's acting like she's in high school now?

At least we got to have pot roast twice in one week. I sighed. Mom's pot roast is awesome.

As soon as everyone was seated Rose reached for the gravy boat. "Where's Lily?" she asked.

"She went to Lindsey's after school," Mom

replied. "Mrs. Underwood offered to drive her home. They were going out for pizza."

"Daisy," said Hal conversationally. "How was the game against Marshfield today?"

"We won," I answered.

"Your record's two and oh?"

Usually I'm happy for a chance to talk about sports, but I didn't feel like it right then. I speared a carrot with my fork. "Yep."

Hal lifted his wineglass. "Well, cheers."

"Yes, cheers." Mom raised her glass, too.

I looked at Mom, not at Hal. "Thanks."

"Hal, I have a question for you," Rose said. "I'm taking an economics class, and I was wondering if you could go over one chapter with me. I absolutely do *not* understand this supply-side stuff."

Hal launched into an economics lecture, which Rose and Mom both listened to as if it were Nobel Prize material. I ate as fast as I could, figuring that the sooner I was excused from the table, the better. As I took one last bite Lily waltzed into the room. "Hi, I'm home," she sang, scooting into a chair. "Any dessert left?"

Mom was gaping. "Lily, what is that on your face?"

We all turned to look at Lily, who blinked innocently at Mom with jet black eyelashes that were about three inches long. Lily's cheeks were unnaturally pink, and I thought I detected lip gloss and eye shadow, too. "Nothing?" Lily answered, but without much conviction.

"March right to the bathroom and wash that off," Mom ordered.

"But Lindsey and Talia and Kendall and Kimberly's moms let them—," Lily began to protest.

"In our house no one under the age of fourteen wears makeup," Mom declared firmly. "To the bathroom. *Now.*"

Lily slid off her chair, her starlet's eyes sullen. As she stomped from the kitchen we could hear her muttering to herself, "I guess you want me to be a loser. . . ."

Mom gave Hal a helpless look. Hal smiled. "I'm glad I had boys," he said.

Mom was scraping plates and I was rinsing them and putting them in the dishwasher when Lily reappeared, her face scrubbed pink and her eyelashes blond once more. "I hope you're satisfied, Mom," she grumbled.

"I'll be satisfied when you promise you won't put on makeup until you're fourteen," Mom replied.

"I promise," Lily said, still pouting.

Mom hugged her.

"You don't need makeup, Lily," Hal said gallantly, carrying a platter over to the counter. "You're pretty as a peach without it."

For a moment Lily looked somewhat mollified. Then her expressive mouth turned upside down again. "Mom, will you help me with my math homework? Mr. Cabot gave us ten absolutely impossible word problems."

"I'll help you," Hal offered. "I'm a whiz at word problems."

I finished scrubbing the roast pan and dried my hands on a dish towel. "I'll be home from the hospital around ten, Mom," I said.

"Drive carefully," she advised, as she'd done every time I'd taken the car since I'd gotten my driver's license two weeks before.

I went upstairs to my room to grab my book bag. On my way out I passed by the living room. There was classical music on the stereo, and Hal and Lily were sitting on the sofa. Hal leaned toward the coffee table and scribbled something on a piece of paper. "You need to turn the word problem into an equation," he told Lily. "Cartoons help."

Lily giggled at whatever Hal was drawing. Mom looked up from the cookbook she was reading to smile at them. Laurel was feeding her goldfish, whose bowl sits on top of an end table—she has hamsters, too, and a turtle. Rose was doing her economics homework. It was a cozy domestic scene . . . and I couldn't wait to get away from it.

Not that I couldn't have used a night off from my job. I was yawning when I checked in with my boss, Jody, the head nurse in the pediatric wing. "Need a cup of coffee?" she offered, looking up from her clipboard as I dumped my book bag on the reception desk.

I shook my head. Mom and Rose both love coffee, but I don't drink much—caffeine's not good for athletes. "Thanks, anyway," I told Jody.

The pediatric wing is lively. Sick kids and their

families are always going in and out, the doctors and nurses are so cheerful it hurts, and the phone rings constantly. Usually I don't mind that, but tonight I was trying to study my trigonometry in between calls. I'd gotten a B-minus on Ms. Stern's first quiz, not a good performance by my usual straight-A standards. Plus the material wasn't even that hard. I just didn't have enough time to study.

The phone buzzed. Pushing aside my math book, I punched line two, lifting the receiver. "Hello? Room three-ten? I'll connect you." It rang again before I'd hung up. I punched line one. "Good evening, Community Hospital Pediatrics. No, Doctor Dimarco isn't on call this evening. Can I transfer you to the head nurse?"

It went on like that for an hour or so. I gave up on math and opened my English assignment. That's when I heard someone ask, "What are you reading?"

I looked up from my book to see a thin teenage boy in sweats smiling down at me. He had on a baseball cap, but it didn't really hide the fact that he was bald.

"F. Scott Fitzgerald," I told him, smiling back. "*The Great Gatsby*. Have you read it?"

"Sure. Since I got sick, I've read just about every book that's ever been written. There's nothing else to do sometimes. I'm Ben," he added, sticking out his hand. "Ben Compton."

"Daisy Walker," I replied as we shook.

Ben pulled up a chair, straddling it backward. "You just started working here, right?"

"Right."

"I noticed because I'm here a lot," he said. "Chemotherapy."

"Oh. So you have . . ."

"Yep, the *C* word." Ben grinned. "Cancer—a brain tumor."

I raised my eyebrows. "This is funny?"

"Sure." He laughed at my shocked expression. "A cosmic joke. You've got to see it that way, or else it's too depressing."

"Well, you look . . ."

"Hairless?"

Now I laughed. "I was just going to say you look good. For someone who's sick," I added.

We smiled at each other. "Okay, so, Daisy, do you go to South Regional?"

"I'm a junior."

"I go to Kent."

"A junior?"

"Sophomore. But thanks."

"It must be tough," I said, "having to miss so much school. Are you keeping up with the work?"

"I'm managing," Ben replied. "The worst part is not being able to do sports."

"What do you play?"

"Soccer and lacrosse."

"Me too," I said. "Soccer, I mean."

"I can't wait to play again. I will, one of these days."

I looked at him, wondering. A brain tumor . . . that was serious. "Yeah?"

"Yeah." He lifted up one skinny arm. "See this?" A frown darkened his face momentarily. "I can't even do one push-up." His expression brightened again. "But in a couple of months I'll be working out again. I'll be arm wrestling everyone on this ward, so watch out."

The phone lit up.

"Excuse me," I said.

"That's okay—I'd better get back to my room, anyway. Don't want them to give my bed away," he joked.

"See you around, Ben."

"You will," he said.

As I picked up the phone I followed Ben with my eyes. From the back he looked like a beanpole, and he shuffled his feet like an old man. He's optimistic if he thinks he'll be working out anytime soon, I thought, an unexpected ache in my heart. But I hope he makes it. I really hope he makes it.

When I'd finished my *Great Gatsby* chapters, I went back to trig, but I didn't make much progress. I would read a line or two, scrawl a couple of figures in my notebook, and then I'd field three calls in a row. Around nine-thirty, though, things quieted down. The pediatric patients were tucked into bed, their relatives had gone home, and the staff settled into night mode: fewer people running around, voices lowered, lights dimmed.

I transferred a call to the nurses' station and then looked back down at my trig book. I flipped back to the previous page, rubbing my eyes. I don't even remember reading this stuff, I thought dismally. If Ms. Stern gave one of her pop quizzes the next day, I was sunk.

I stared at the book, pencil in hand, ready to copy out a problem. Blinking, I tried to focus on the tiny print. A minute or two later I woke up with a start because the phone buzzed right next to my ear. I'd dozed off, my head dropping onto the open book. "Community Hospital Pediatrics," I mumbled into the receiver. "How may I direct your call?"

After I hung up the phone, I glanced hopefully at the clock on the wall, but its hands were moving with discouraging slowness. Twenty minutes to go, and I wasn't sure I could keep my eyes open that long. Maybe Mom was right, I thought. Maybe I don't really need this job. If I'm already feeling stressed out after just two weeks . . .

No way am I quitting, though, I decided a split second later. The money would really help. Besides, my life had always been a juggling act—I just had one more ball to keep in the air now. I could do it.

I sat up straighter in my chair, stretching my arms over my head. Then I hopped to my feet and did a couple of jumping jacks. I waved to Jody at the nurses' station. "I'll take that cup of coffee after all," I called.

"Black or with cream and sugar?" she asked.

"Black," I replied.

By the time I got home, the caffeine had really kicked in and I was feeling a little jittery. I had a

sinking feeling the coffee strategy was going to
backfire and that I'd have trouble falling asleep.
Well, if that were the case, I could put my insomnia
to good use and finish my trig assignment, maybe
even get a jump on my homework. I was only a
third of the way through *The Great Gatsby*, with my
first English paper due in less than a week.

"Good, Daisy, you're home," Mom said as soon
as I stepped through the door.

"What's up?" I asked, hanging my denim jacket
on the coatrack in the front hall.

"Come into the kitchen—I want to show you
something," she replied.

I followed her into the kitchen. Mom waved at
the table. My eyes widened. "A computer," I exclaimed. "Wow! Where'd that come from?"

"It was Hal's. He bought a new laptop and says
he never uses this one anymore. It's for all of us,"
Mom explained. "I'm going to put my business
records on it, and you girls can use it for homework
It has a built-in modem, too, so we can hook up to
the Internet. Isn't that great?"

I nodded wordlessly.

"So, Hal gave me this manual," Mom said, lifting a glossy-covered notebook, "but I'm having a
hard time understanding it. You took that computer
course in school last year. Do you think you could
help me figure out—"

"It's Hal's computer and Hal's manual," I
snapped. "Why don't you ask *him* to help you?"

Mom stared at me in surprise. I was instantly

overcome with shame. I never talked back to her, never used a snotty tone like that, and I hated myself for doing it. What is it about Hal that's driving me crazy? I wondered. The computer was a generous gift. "Mom, I'm sorry," I said. "I'm just tired. And I had a cup of coffee at work and I just feel . . . tired," I said again. "I'm sorry."

"It's okay." Her eyebrows pulled together in a frown. "I'm worried about you, Daisy. You need to get more sleep."

"I'm going to bed right now," I told her, crossing the room to give her a quick hug. "Unless you want to look over the computer manual together."

"No, go to bed," she insisted, giving me a gentle push toward the door. "We can work on it tomorrow."

"Right," I said. "There'll be time tomorrow."

There wasn't time tomorrow, or the next day, or the next. Days used to be so long, I thought one afternoon as I dressed for soccer practice. Was it something about turning sixteen? All of a sudden there weren't enough hours in the day for all the things I needed to do. I felt like I was constantly rushing from one activity to the next, shortchanging all of them. "My paper on *The Great Gatsby* stunk," I told Kristin and Jamila as we walked out to the field.

"It had to have been better than mine," said Kristin, her arms lifted to weave her long red hair into a braid. She's in Mrs. Rogowski's section. "I got a B."

"I got a C," I said, grimacing.

"*You* got a C? You always ace your English papers," Jamila said.

"Not this one. It was supposed to be five pages long, right? I only turned in three and a half. And almost half of that was my topic sentence, which just rambled on and on because I had no idea what I was trying to say. Mr. Kamin nailed me on it."

"At least he lets you do rewrites," Kristin said. "Mrs. Rogowski doesn't." She tipped her face to the sky. "Hey, isn't it a great day for soccer practice?"

It was the first day of October. The sky was a soft blue, and a warm Indian summer breeze stirred the leaves on the trees bordering the field, leaves just beginning to turn yellow and orange.

"Yeah, the weather's nice, but Wheeler's going to work our butts off," said Jamila. "Eastport's the toughest game of the season."

We had an away game the next day at a high school half an hour up the coast. Eastport always had a strong team, and the captain of their team, the Chiefs, was a senior named Lisa Levison, who had been an All New England forward for two years in a row. "We can beat them, though," Kristin declared with confidence. "They have Lisa Levison, but we have Daisy Walker."

"Our not so secret weapon," Jamila agreed, flashing me a smile.

Usually I like a little pressure—the higher people's expectations, the better I perform. But right then it was as if I had two left feet. Jamila beat me in the wind sprints, and I missed four out of five shots on goal during the scoring drill. Every other ball I touched ended up out-of-bounds. After forty-five minutes we took a water break and Coach Wheeler took me aside. "Hey, Daisy, what's up?"

"I'm thirsty," I said.

He handed me a bottle, and I squirted some sports drink into my mouth. "That's all?" he asked.

"A little tired, too," I admitted, although exhausted would have been a more accurate term. "I stayed up late studying."

"Don't do that tonight," he counseled, "or Levison will be all over you tomorrow."

"Don't worry," I replied. "I'll be hot. You can count on me."

"I know I can," he said, giving me a swat on the back.

"I'll outscore Levison two to one," I vowed.

"That's the spirit."

We rejoined the rest of the team, and practice resumed. For some reason I felt sort of let down. It had been too easy to reassure Coach Wheeler. Why hadn't he pressed me a little harder? But even if he had, could I have told him what was really bothering me since I don't know myself? I wondered.

No, I'd given him the right answer. My coach and team could depend on me. I never let them down. I never let anyone down.

"Okay, the Chiefs are on top but only by one goal," Coach Wheeler said the following day as our team huddled during halftime. "I know the weather isn't helping, but we can turn things around if you put your hearts into it. Play the way you played against Kent and Marshfield. Uh, Walker."

He turned to me, his expression solemn. Rain dripped from the bill of his baseball cap. I was leaning against Jamila, both of us shivering under one raincoat. Overnight, Indian summer had fled, and the drizzle was icy but not bad enough to call the game.

"Yes?" I answered.

"I'm putting Maria in."

Maria Galdamez is the second-string forward, my backup. Maria blinked at me in surprise; I blinked at Coach Wheeler. "You're benching me?" I asked in disbelief.

"Resting you," he corrected. "I think you need it."

My face flooded with color. I hadn't had the best first half, it was true. The night before, I'd worked at the hospital until ten, then stayed up late rewriting my *Great Gatsby* paper. "Give me five minutes," I begged Coach Wheeler. "If I don't score, you can take me out."

"This isn't just about goals, Daisy." He shook his head. "It's about knowing when one of my players needs a break."

"I'm fine," I insisted. "I just needed to warm up. Please, Coach. Five minutes."

He frowned, looking me up and down. "Well ...," he said finally. "Okay. You've got five minutes to show me that all you need to do is warm up, but that's it."

The referee blew her whistle: It was time to start the third quarter. As I trotted back onto the field I heard Coach Wheeler say to Maria, "Stretch out a little—do a few sprints. I want you to be ready, okay?"

I gritted my teeth. I had nothing against Maria. She was a nice kid, and with more experience she'd be a good player. She can have my position, I thought, *after* I graduate.

In the center of the field I stood face-to-face with Lisa Levison. Neither of us smiled. The ball was set down on the wet grass, and our bodies tensed with readiness. Then the whistle blew.

What had Coach Wheeler said? We could win if we put our hearts into it? I put my heart into it, and my bones and muscles and guts. I wasn't playing smart—I was too tired for that. I was playing mad.

The ball bounced wildly around the field. First Eastport had possession, then we did, then Eastport again. Then Jamila dove into the action, tackled the ball away from the Chiefs' left wing, and kicked it sharply in my direction. This was my chance.

I sprinted toward the goal, pushing the ball just ahead of me as I ran. I zigzagged past the Eastport defense, dodging and pivoting, the ball glued to my cleats. I wasn't going to lose it, not on my life. I heard Kristin shout to me, "I'm open!" It was a good chance to pass, but I didn't take it. I kept the ball even though there were two Eastport defensive players between me and the goal. I feinted left, then sprinted to the right and went for the shot.

The angle was crazy. As I kicked the ball I had to twist my body to face the goal, and my left foot skidded on the wet grass. The ball flew wide, and I fell hard to the ground.

The pain in my left knee was so intense that for a few seconds I had to lie with my eyes closed. Then Coach Wheeler's voice penetrated the buzzing in my ears. "Take it easy," he said as I struggled to sit up. "What is it, your knee?"

I nodded, biting my lip.

"Yeah, look at that," he said. "It's as big as a cantaloupe already." He turned to yell over his shoulder to the Eastport coach. "Hey, let's get a trainer out here!"

"I'm okay," I lied. "Help me, you guys." Jamila and Kristin knelt down next to me, and I wrapped my arms around their shoulders. They lifted me up and I stood, balancing on my right foot. "See?" I said, my face pale from the pain. "No sweat." When I tried to take a step, though, tears rushed into my eyes. I couldn't bear any weight on my left leg.

Coach Wheeler helped Jamila and Kristin carry me over to the bench, and the Eastport trainer wrapped my knee in ice. While the game started up again, with Maria taking my place, Coach Wheeler called the hospital on his cellular phone. I could hear him mumbling. "Possibly ligament damage. An MRI? Take a look at her first. No, I'm not sure about insurance. Okay. We'll be there in thirty minutes."

Coach Wheeler sat down next to me on the bench. "I'm going to call your mom and have her meet us at the emergency room."

"It's not that bad," I said, but I couldn't keep the tears from spilling down my cheeks.

Coach Wheeler put an arm around my shoulders, giving me a silent hug.

We'd all driven up on a school bus, so Coach Wheeler and I had to borrow a van from the Eastport athletic department in order to get me to the community hospital. I went there all the time for my job, but it was different being the injured person lying on a gurney in the ER. Scarier.

A couple of nurses—no one I knew—were wheeling me into an examining room when Coach Wheeler got a call on his cellular phone. "Uh-huh, uh-huh," he mumbled.

He clicked off the phone. "The team lost," he reported to me. "Five–four."

An ER resident in powder blue scrubs started asking me and Coach Wheeler questions about how I'd hurt my knee. I let my coach answer—I could hardly speak because my throat was choked up with pain and frustration. How could I have been such a klutz? I thought bitterly. I should have stayed on my feet and scored that goal. If I'd been out there till the end, we'd have won.

But I couldn't rewind the tape. The game was over.

F o u r

"Three *months?*" I practically shouted the words, my voice shrill with disbelief.

The day after I'd fallen during the soccer game against Eastport, I was back at the hospital, sitting on an examining table in Dr. Thigpen's office, with my injured leg stretched out in front of me. Mom was there, too, and we'd just finished looking at my MRI.

"You'll need crutches for a few weeks," Dr. Thigpen said, his tone soothing. "But torn ligaments take a while to heal. Here's the bright side—you'll probably want to do some physical therapy down the road, but you don't need surgery."

Mom squeezed my hand. "That's good news," she said.

I shook my head. "But three months. That means . . . I'm out for the rest of the soccer season."

Dr. Thigpen nodded. "I'm afraid so."

I'd suspected this but hadn't wanted to believe it. "What about basketball this winter?"

Dr. Thigpen looked down at my swollen knee. "You'll be getting around a lot more easily in a few months, but you probably won't be in shape for

43

basketball. That's one of the toughest sports on knees. By spring, though, you should be back in business. What do you play in the spring?"

"Softball," I said weakly. Spring seemed about a million years away. "Shortstop."

"Hey, I played shortstop for *my* high school baseball team," Dr. Thigpen told me with a chummy smile.

"No kidding," I said.

We talked for a few more minutes about icing my knee and stuff like that, then made an appointment for me to come back in two weeks. Dr. Thigpen sent me off with a pair of crutches and a pat on the back.

As we were leaving the hospital we bumped into Jody, the head nurse on the ward where I worked. "Daisy, what *happened?*" she exclaimed.

I told her the whole gruesome story. Jody gave me a hug. "We like you so much, we were hoping we could find a way to get you to spend more time here, but this isn't what I had in mind," she said with a rueful smile. "Take care of yourself, Daisy, okay?"

Mom was chatty and upbeat as we made our way slowly to the parking lot, but I wasn't really listening to what she was saying. Dr. Thigpen's words were still echoing in my head. *Three months, three months, three months . . .*

I called Jamila as soon as I got home from the doctor's. "That's terrible," she groaned when she heard the verdict. "What are we going to do without you?"

"You guys'll be fine." I sniffled, feeling very sorry for myself. "You and Kristen have always been the backbone of the team, anyway. And Maria will learn fast. She has a lot of talent."

"She's not in your league," Jamila said. "Besides, it's not just about how good you are. You're our best bud. I miss you already!"

I let Jamila say some more nice things about me because it made me feel less depressed, and then I hung up and limped on my crutches down the hall. I headed for the kitchen, figuring I'd see if I could set the table hopping on one foot, but when I heard Mom and Hal's voices, I detoured into the living room instead. "It's going to be rough on her," Hal was saying about somebody. *Me*, I guessed.

"I know," Mom agreed. There was a brief whirring noise—the food processor. "Sports are a big part of who she is," Mom went on. Something sizzled in a skillet. Chopped onions? "But if it had to happen to any of the girls—of course I wish that it *hadn't* happened—but if it had to happen, Daisy's the one who can handle it. She's got the right attitude. Nothing ever gets her down. Even when Jim died, she kept her chin up. I've often wished I had some of her optimism!"

I decided to let someone else set the table and hopped quietly back to my room. So that's what other people thought of me. "Daisy can handle it. . . . the right attitude . . . Nothing ever gets her down. . . ." Is that really how I seemed to the world? Tears stung my eyes. Didn't Mom know how hard it was to be strong and cheerful sometimes? *Acting* happy and *feeling* happy are two totally different things.

By the time I got back to my room, I was out of breath from the effort of using the crutches. Tossing them on the floor, I flopped on my bed, my knee throbbing painfully. Maybe I'm tired of keeping my chin up, I thought, closing my eyes.

The next day after school I sat slumped forward on the bleachers, watching my soccer teammates practice. It was weird to be wearing jeans and a sweater instead of cleats and sweats. I kept wanting to run down and jump into the drills, but then I'd remember my knee. Not that I could really forget it. I was taking painkillers, but it still ached.

I'd thought sitting in on practice would make me feel like I was still part of things, and everybody did come over to talk to me and ask how I felt, which was nice. But when Kristin dropped me off at home later, I felt even more depressed than before. I dragged myself into the apartment and collapsed in a kitchen chair, groaning out loud.

Rose was eating a container of yogurt and reading her sociology textbook. "You look like death," she observed.

"Thanks for the moral support," I said dryly.

Rose put down her book. "I know exactly how you feel," she said. "Remember last May, when I got laryngitis and couldn't be in the spring musical?"

"Yeah, but it didn't take you three *months* to get better," I pointed out.

"True," she admitted. "Cheer up, though, okay? I mean, what will happen to this family if Suzy Sunshine turns into Suzy Storm Cloud?"

Rose was trying to get me to smile, but I didn't have anything to smile about. Not today, anyway. *Suzy Sunshine?* I thought. *Make that Suzy Sidelined.*

"Welcome to the club," Ben Compton said when I hobbled over to his hospital room to say hi my first day back on the job.

He and I had been talking a bunch of times, and I was starting to really like him. Ben knew some hilarious jokes because he surfed the Net a lot. We found out that we both collected baseball cards, so we'd done some trading—in spite of the fact that he always tried to swindle me.

"What club?" I asked him now.

"The club of ex-soccer players," Ben replied.

I was standing at the door to his room, which was in a separate oncology section of the pediatric wing. He was in the midst of heavy-duty chemotherapy and his immune system was suppressed, so he wasn't supposed to have visitors other than his family. To be perfectly honest, he looked pretty bad. "I can't come in, huh?"

"Unless you want to put on a mask and gown."

"It's just kind of hard to hear you from over here," I told him.

Ben cleared his throat. "Better?"

His voice was still kind of faint and scratchy, but I said, "Yes."

"It stinks, doesn't it?" he remarked. His eyes were half closed, and his skin was yellowish and blotchy. "But at least you know you'll be back to normal. I'll never get out of this damned bed."

Ben's condition definitely put my relatively minor problem in perspective. He was usually cheerful, though, and I had never heard him sound so negative. For a moment I didn't know what to say.

I fell back on this joke about the self-pity police. "Here they come," I said, certain he'd know what I was talking about. "They're going to arrest you."

Ben cracked a weak smile. "Couldn't you be a little nicer to a dying man?"

My stomach gave an involuntary lurch at the word *dying*, but I tried not to show it. "No way, José. Snap out of it."

"All right, all right." He smiled weakly.

A nurse appeared at my shoulder. "Ben needs to rest," she advised me.

I didn't really want to go, but it didn't look like I had much choice. "Okay. Bye, Ben. Hang in there."

I waved, and he managed to lift a hand from the sheet in response. "Like I have an alternative."

I had to watch out for the self-pity police myself a day later. For the first time in memory, I didn't have anything to do after school. I had decided not to watch the team practice anymore—it made me too sad. On Friday afternoon I rode the school bus home, but the apartment was empty. Mom was out, Laurel and Lily both had after-school activities, and Rose had gone to the Greyhound station, duffel in hand, to catch a bus to Boston—she was visiting Stephen at Harvard for the weekend. I didn't feel like sitting around by myself, even though I had a ton of homework, so I headed back out on my crutches.

It was a gray October day, and the low, dark sky matched my mood. Leaning heavily on my crutches, I limped along the sidewalk, window shopping. Did I feel like a cookie from Wissinger's Bakery? Nah, I wasn't hungry, and besides, now that I couldn't exercise much, I'd have to watch my weight. There was a sale at Harrington's Department Store and also at Cecilia's, but I didn't need new clothes and couldn't afford them anyhow. I hobbled past Appleby's Hardware Store and the Down East News and Drugstore and Patsy's Diner and the Corner Ice Cream Shoppe. When I got to the end of the commercial part of town, I stopped.

For a few minutes I just stood on one foot at the corner of Main Street and Lighthouse Road. I didn't have a destination. I felt adrift, and that scared me. It was like something at the center of my life had been torn away, something that held the rest together.

A nursery rhyme popped into my head. *Humpty-Dumpty sat on a wall, Humpty-Dumpty had a great fall. All the king's horses and all the king's men . . .*

Who's going to put *me* back together? I wondered as I turned around and limped back toward home.

F i v e

I'm not *totally* helpless," I told Mom a week later. "The car's an automatic, and it's my left leg that's hurt—I can still drive. Besides, it would give me something to do."

Mom studied me, arms folded. "Are you sure?"

I nodded. "I'm sure."

"Well, it would be a big help," she admitted, fishing in her purse for her keys. "I need to get started on this wedding cake because I'm catering the cocktail party, too, and that noisy muffler's been driving me crazy. And tell them the engine light's blinking on and off and have them change the oil, too, okay?"

Mom called ahead to Dave's Fuel 'n' Fix to tell them I was bringing the car in. They told her they could look at it right away, so I took along my backpack—I figured I'd do some homework while I was waiting.

The station wasn't busy, and the mechanic, a burly middle-aged guy named Ralph, had the car up on blocks in no time. I settled down on a bench in front of the service station, my crutches propped against the wall, and pulled my history book out of my pack. I didn't open it right away, though; I just

51

held it on my lap while I tipped my face to the sky, the autumn sun warm on my skin.

I think I was starting to snore when an amused voice jolted me from my daydreams. "Hey, Sleeping Beauty."

I opened my eyes and blinked. A tall, thin guy about my age stood in front of me, blocking the sunlight. He was wearing a shirt with the name Peter embroidered over the chest pocket. His sandy hair was longish—he had a couple of dreadlocks on one side and a pierced ear with a little silver hoop in it. That kind of alterna-look wasn't usually my thing, but his sharp-featured face was handsome, and for some reason I found myself blushing. "Um, are you talking to me?" I asked.

"Do you see anyone else here?" he asked, smiling. He put one foot up on my bench and leaned his crossed forearms on his knee, gazing down at me. His eyes were intensely blue. "You're Daisy, right? Ralph just sent me to tell you that the car'll be about forty-five more minutes."

"Oh. Okay," I said, adding, "um, yeah, I'm Daisy. And you're . . . Peter."

"My friends call me Paco."

"How come?"

"I have no idea."

We both laughed. "You, uh, work here?" I asked. I don't usually come up with such dumb questions, but this guy was so cute, he was affecting my brain.

"Just since last week." A smile lingered in his eyes. "In case you were wondering why you hadn't noticed me before."

Dave's was the only gas station in Hawk Harbor, and I *had* been wondering that. I blushed again. "Pumping gas?" I asked lamely.

"Pumping gas," he confirmed. "Lucky for me, Hawk Harbor still hasn't heard of self-serve."

Just then a red pickup truck pulled up to the pump. "Back in a minute," Peter said, and walked over to it. "Fill 'er with regular," I heard the driver say.

I watched as Peter moved around the truck, cleaning the windows with the squeegee. He had the easy stride of an athlete, and that got me wondering again. When the pickup drove off, he took the ten-dollar bill inside to the cash register, then rejoined me on the bench. "You don't go to South Regional," I guessed.

Peter shook his head. "Nah. I went to Kent High for a while, but I got kicked out."

I was intrigued. "Really?"

"It wasn't my scene," he said with a careless shrug.

"Does your family live in Kent?"

"We used to, but now we're bunking with my aunt in Hawk Harbor. It's just me and my mom. My dad bailed when I was in kindergarten."

"Wow. That's awful."

"Yeah, apparently he was a bum," Peter said. "I don't remember him, to tell you the truth."

I thought about my own lost father. I remembered every single thing about him. "That must've been rough on your mother."

"Sure, and now she has MS—multiple sclerosis.

So she's sick on and off, can't hold down a job. That's why we're freeloading off Aunt Trish."

"Wow," I said again. "That must be really hard."

"Life deals some people a lousy hand," Peter agreed.

Another car pulled in and he hopped up. After he'd tallied up the sale, he came back outside again. This time he was carrying a guitar. Without speaking, he sat down next to me and started strumming. "What's that?" I asked, pointing to something on his finger that looked like a glass thimble.

"A slide. So you can get sounds like this." He played a quick riff.

The notes were liquid and beautiful. "It sounds like a voice," I told him. "Like singing."

"It does, doesn't it?"

Bending his head, he played for a minute. Then he stopped abruptly, clapping his hand against the strings to silence them, and looked straight at me. "What were you playing?" I asked.

"Don't know. Haven't given it a name yet."

My eyes widened. "You *wrote* that?"

"Yeah," he said dismissively. "It's nothing."

"I thought it was really pretty."

"Well." He smiled slowly. "Then maybe I'll call it 'Daisy's Song.'"

I blushed yet again. Peter put the guitar down. He stretched his arms over his head, yawning, and his shirt lifted up a little, exposing a narrow strip of flat, sun-browned abdominals. I shifted my eyes away, wondering if it were possible for my face to get any pinker.

"Kind of slow right now, huh?" Peter observed,

gazing at the vacant gas pumps. "And Ralph's still working on your car. How about you and me"—he paused suggestively as my throat tightened—"play a game of chess?"

"Chess?" I laughed. "Are you joking?"

"Nope. Got a portable set inside. You wait right here."

When Peter brought the chess set out and opened up the board, I confessed that I'd never played. He explained the rules to me, and we played a couple of short games. Needless to say, it didn't take him many moves to trounce me. "I'll never get the hang of this," I said with a laugh as he seized my queen.

"Sure, you will," Peter said. "You play soccer, right?" I'd told him how I hurt my leg. "It's the same kind of thing. You have to think ahead, visualize how the game will unfold, how the players will move. Let your brain roam over the possibilities."

I shook my head, smiling. "I think that might be harder than it sounds."

Inside the garage I saw Ralph waving at me. It looked like my car was done, but I wasn't in a rush to leave. When will I see this guy again? I wondered with a strange urgency. My family didn't do that much driving—we wouldn't need another fill-up for a week or so. "So, since you live in Hawk Harbor now, do you think you'll enroll at school?" I asked Peter.

Peter packed away the chess pieces. "Doubtful. I'd just get kicked out again. I have, like, every learning disability in the book, supposedly. You know, lots of 'potential,' but I could never quite follow the rules. Anyhow," he added, his eyes glued to mine, "there are better ways to learn what the world has to teach."

"Oh. Right. I know what you mean," I said, even though I didn't.

I paid for the car repair with the blank check Mom had given me, and then Peter helped me into the driver's seat. It was a little awkward—I couldn't bend my left leg all the way because of the brace.

I rolled down the window. "See you around . . . uh . . . Paco," I said, trying not to sound too hopeful.

"You bet," he replied.

As I pulled onto the road I glanced in my rearview mirror. Peter was watching me drive away. He lifted a hand in a casual wave, and I hit the horn.

I don't usually spend that much time thinking about the opposite sex—I'm not boy crazy like Rose, or like she was before she settled down with Stephen. But I thought about Peter all the way home . . . and until dinner . . . and after dinner until I went to bed. Then, even though I usually sleep like a log, I saw him in my dreams.

The next Sunday morning Mom dragged us all out of bed to go to church. I have to admit that during Reverend Beecher's sermon, I was still picturing Peter, playing the slide guitar and stretching his arms over his head in a yawn.

When we got home, my sisters and I crowded into the kitchen to make brunch—since Mom cooks for a living, we give her a break whenever we can. Lily mixed the waffle batter while Laurel haphazardly sliced apples into a saucepan for applesauce. Rose threw in a load of laundry—the washer and dryer are in a closet off the kitchen—and I set the table, hopping on one foot.

"It's eleven. Do you think it's too early to call Stephen at school?" Rose asked me as she sorted the lights from the darks. She answered her own question before I could. "Yeah, I'm sure he's sleeping in—there was probably a party last night. Or two or three parties."

She sounded disapproving. "Didn't you go to a bunch of parties last weekend when you were down there?" I asked. "I thought you said it was a blast."

"It was." Rose twisted the dial on the washing machine. "But I'm not there this weekend. You know?"

"Maybe you should just tell Stephen you expect him to stay in his room with his nose in a book when you're not there," I said.

"I don't think he'd go for it." She sighed. "You should see that campus. It's incredibly gorgeous and crawling with pretty girls. Pretty *and* brainy."

"No one's smarter or prettier than you," I reminded her. "Yeah," said Lily. "Remember what it said in the yearbook last year? You got 'Best Smile' *and* 'Most Talented.'"

Rose frowned. "Anyone can be a big fish in a small pond. South Regional's not exactly Harvard."

"I still wouldn't worry," I said. "When's Stephen going to come home for a visit?"

"Probably never," Rose said, obviously determined not to be cheered up. "Why would he, when he's having so much fun at school?"

I finished setting the table and retrieved my crutches. "Need help?" I asked my younger sisters.

"Would you get me the cinnamon?" Laurel replied.

I grabbed a jar from the spice rack. "Is Jack coming over?" I asked her.

Laurel sprinkled some cinnamon on the apples. "I doubt it."

"How come? He never misses waffles."

Laurel gave the applesauce an impatient stir. "Since I said no, he asked another girl in our class to go out with him. Tammy Nickerson," she added with a sniff.

"The one who started wearing a bra in, like, third grade?" Rose asked.

Laurel nodded grimly. "Yep."

"Couldn't you still invite him over for brunch?" I wondered.

Laurel shook her head. "You can't hang out with another girl when you're going out with someone," she informed me in a duh-don't-you-know-anything? tone. "He's probably having brunch with Tammy."

"You sound like you're sorry you turned him down when he asked *you* to go out with him," Rose remarked.

"I am not," Laurel declared. "Absolutely, totally not!"

I raised my eyebrows at Rose. "Oh," Rose said to Laurel. "I see."

*   *   *

Jack didn't make it to brunch, but Hal did. "Great waffles," he said, piling his plate high. "You made these, Lily?"

Lily nodded, pleased. "Yep. Cooking talent runs in the family."

Hal chuckled. I tried not to gag. For once Mom wasn't smiling, either. Leaning her elbows on the table, she looked at Lily. "Lily, were you using the computer last night?"

Lily blinked at Mom's tone. I could almost see her thinking, Is this a trick question? "Um . . ."

"Because someone erased one of my files—my budget for the catering business."

Lily's face turned a guilty red. "Oh. I didn't mean to—"

"You know you're not supposed to go into my files," Mom said.

"Well, I was on the Internet," Lily explained. "You know, in that chat room? And then it started to get really stupid, so I decided to write a story, and I accidentally clicked on your file instead, and I don't know how it happened, but—"

"You better not have been snooping in *my* files," Rose cut in.

"You mean the one with the letters you write to Stephen?" Lily asked. "No, I'd never—"

"And that's another thing," Mom said. "This chat room business." She looked at Hal. "Lily and her friends spend an awful lot of time that way, on week-nights, too, when they should be doing homework."

"Well, if you're worried about it," said Hal,

"maybe you should consider limiting the time Lily spends in chat rooms to, say, twenty minutes a night." Mom nodded, and Hal went on, "And maybe she should forfeit her computer privileges for a while if she can't learn to respect privacy."

I couldn't believe Hal—who did he think he was? "Didn't you hear her say it was an accident?" I spoke up, my eyes flashing. "And *Mom* makes the rules around here!"

"Daisy!" Mom said, surprised.

"Well, I just think . . ." I swallowed the rest of the angry words that threatened to spill out. *What was the matter with me?* Dad would have been furious at rude behavior like that. "I think I'll have another waffle," I finished.

Mom didn't let it go at that. When brunch was over, Hal went to see if he could recover Mom's lost computer file. My sisters took off, leaving me with the dishes. As I rinsed off the plates and put them in the dishwasher, balancing awkwardly on my good leg, Mom poured another cup of coffee and gave me a little lecture. "I didn't like your manners when you were talking to Hal," she told me. "You spoke out of turn."

Even though I knew she had a point, I couldn't stand to talk about it. "*I* spoke out of turn?" I countered. "I thought Hal did. It's not his place to tell us how to act. He's not our father."

Mom didn't respond. For a minute she sipped her coffee, her eyebrows furrowed and her jaw tense. Then she left the kitchen.

* * *

I worked at the hospital from 2 until 8 P.M. on Sunday. It was a good shift. Ben was doing better, and I spent a good chunk of time chatting with him.

Heading home, I found myself taking a detour. I was feeling so good, I felt like having an adventure. Instead of driving straight back to the apartment on Main Street, I turned down the Old Boston Post Road and pulled into Dave's Fuel 'n' Fix.

I didn't really need gas—I still had half a tank. And he might not even be working tonight.

When I spotted Peter, my heart rate doubled. *What if he doesn't remember me?* I thought as I rolled down the window.

He remembered me. "Fill 'er up, Sleeping Beauty?" he asked, giving me a slow smile.

"Yes. Thanks," I said somewhat breathlessly.

Peter filled up the tank—I only needed three gallons—and I paid him. I hesitated with my right hand on the key in the ignition. I couldn't just drive away. I wanted something to happen. My tongue was tied in a knot, though. *How do you make the first move?* I wondered, wishing for the first time in my life that I knew how to flirt.

As it turned out, I didn't need to make the first move. Opening the door on the other side of my car, Peter climbed into the passenger seat. "I'm off work as of now," he told me. "Want to go to a party?"

"It's a school night," I pointed out.

He grinned. "So?"

"So . . ." I thought about all the homework I still had to do. I thought about Mom waiting for me at home. Mom . . . and Hal. "So nothing," I said. "Let's go."

The party was at Peter's friend Zeke's house on Forest Road, on the inland edge of town. The music was so loud that we could hear it as we parked the car by the curb. "I guess Zeke's parents aren't home," I said.

"Zeke's parents are out of it," Peter answered. "We could tear the whole house down and they probably wouldn't notice."

I leaned on my crutches and hopped toward the house. Peter went right in without knocking, and I followed him.

The living room was cloudy with smoke. Kids were flopped on the furniture, some with cigarettes in their hands, others holding plastic cups. Beer? I wondered. "Paco!" someone shouted.

"Hey," he yelled back. "This is Daisy."

A couple of people waved; one guy lifted his cup. A girl with short blue hair standing near the stereo turned the volume even louder. "My favorite song," she screamed in explanation.

Peter introduced me around, but I couldn't hear any of the names over the screeching music. I made some mental notes, though. The girl with the blue hair is with the guy in the tie-dyed shirt, I decided. And the guy with the tattoos must be Zeke.

Peter put his arm around me and steered me into the kitchen. The music wasn't as loud there— we could actually hear each other. "How about a beer?" he asked.

"I don't really drink," I told him.

"Really?" His sandy eyebrows shot up. "Well, that's cool, I guess. Is it, like, a health thing?"

None of my friends drink—we're underage. But then, so was Peter. I didn't want to sound like a loser, so I said, "Yeah."

"How about food, then? Are you hungry?" Peter opened the refrigerator and bent over to peer inside.

"I'm not really—"

Peter was already slapping together a couple of ham-and-cheese sandwiches. "Let's find someplace we can talk," he suggested.

I nodded. "Okay."

We ended up sitting in the upstairs hall with two boys and a girl whom I recognized from South Regional. Although needless to say, we didn't usually hang out in the same crowd. "Daisy's a jock," Peter reported, biting into his sandwich.

"It sure looks like you got over it," the girl named Amy remarked, pointing at my crutches.

Everybody laughed. "I kind of wrecked my knee," I explained.

"It's just as well because exercise is, like, really bad for you," said a guy named Marcus. "I read that somewhere."

"It's much better to exercise your brain," the other guy, Kirk, agreed.

"Like in this fascinating conversation we're having?" Peter asked. Everyone laughed again.

I slumped against the wall, my injured leg stretched out in front of me. We talked about music for a while, then switched to TV shows and movies. Kirk, Marcus, and Amy were funny—they didn't take anything seriously. At one point I said to Amy, "You're in Mr. Kamin's English class, right? Have you started that Mark Twain paper yet?"

"Are you kidding?" Amy laughed. "It's not even on my radar screen. It's due, when, Thursday? I *might* read the book Wednesday night. Or at least the back cover."

Peter disappeared for a minute. When he came back, he had a guitar. I guessed it was Zeke's. For half an hour we played Name That Tune—he'd pick out a few notes, and we'd shout out the song title. Then I happened to get a look at my watch. Ten forty-five! "I have to get home," I told Peter, struggling to my feet. "Do you need a ride anywhere?"

"I think I'll hang out here," he replied, putting down the guitar, "but I'll walk you to your car."

Outside, we stood for a moment next to the car. I jingled the keys nervously, not sure what to do or say. I didn't have that much dating experience . . . and had this even been a date?

"Thanks for inviting me to the party," I said at last, immediately wanting to kick myself for sounding like such a priss.

"Glad you could join me," Peter replied, smiling at our formality.

I hesitated before getting into the car. Peter lifted a hand, lightly touching my hair. "This is really cool hair," he said. "And it's real."

I laughed. "Believe it or not."

"It was good to see you, Sleeping Beauty." Bending forward, he kissed my cheek.

"Um, yeah," I said. "Bye."

"Bye."

I was lucky I didn't run into a police car, or I definitely would have gotten pulled over. I was weaving a little—I kept wandering over the yellow centerline. Peter's kiss had made me dizzy—and it wasn't even on the lips!

At home I crutched into the front hall, heading straight for my room. Mom's voice stopped me before I got to the stairs. "Daisy, is that you?"

I backtracked to the kitchen. Mom was sitting at the table in her bathrobe and slippers. "I was worried about you," she told me, frowning. "I expected you home at eight."

"I know," I mumbled. "I went out after work."

"You should have called."

"I know," I said again.

"Either way, it's almost eleven and your weeknight curfew is ten."

"Sorry."

"Where were you?"

"Just at this guy's house, with someone I met the other day." I yawned. "I'm going to bed. See you tomorrow."

I could tell Mom didn't like my evasiveness—she was still frowning—but I left before she could ask more questions. In my room I dropped my crutches on the floor, then hopped around on one foot, getting ready for bed.

Crawling under the covers, I thought about the evening. Usually I'm careful not to make Mom mad—she has enough to worry about without that hassle. And usually she and I talk about pretty much everything. We've always gotten along really well. But for some reason I didn't feel like talking to her about Peter. Maybe it's because I'm sixteen now, I thought sleepily. Things are going to change. I put a hand to my face, where Peter had kissed me. At least, I hoped so.

S i x

When Melissa came up to me on Wednesday, I was in the cafeteria. Waiting for Jamila and Kristin, I'd bumped into Amy, the girl I'd met at Zeke's party, and we got in the lunch line together. Melissa gave Amy a funny look, and I could tell she was wondering why I was talking to someone with a butterfly tattoo on her forearm, a pack of cigarettes in her pocket, and six pierces in her ear.

"Daisy, hi," Melissa said. "You haven't stopped by the student council office yet. You're going to run, aren't you?"

Amy cocked one eyebrow. "You're thinking about joining the Establishment?" she asked sardonically.

Suddenly it occurred to me that Amy might tell Peter about this conversation. He didn't even *go* to school—would he think running for student council was totally dorky? "Just thinking about it," I said to Amy with studied nonchalance. "I still haven't made up my mind, Mel. How much more time do I have?"

"We're printing the ballots next Monday," Mel answered. "I really hope you run, Daisy."

"I'll sleep on it, okay?" I told Mel.

"Okay." She gave Amy a polite smile. "See you around."

Amy and I moved up in the lunch line. Jamila and Kristin still hadn't appeared—sometimes Coach Wheeler called a short team meeting during lunch, and I figured that was where they were—so Amy helped me with my tray since I was using crutches. We both took sloppy joes and french fries. "Are you really going to run for class president?" Amy asked, laughing. She reached for an orange. "So you can, like, pick the theme for the prom and other important stuff?"

I laughed, too, to show that I didn't take myself too seriously. "I probably won't bother," I said.

"Yeah, because what's the point?" Amy asked.

"Right," I agreed. "What's the point?"

Wednesday after school I went to a girls' varsity soccer home game against Lewisborough. I'd been to all the games, and sometimes I watched part of practice, too—just to stay in touch. Today, though, I wasn't really paying attention to the action on the field even though Jamila scored a hat trick—three goals—and the Sharks won 5–4.

After the game the team took showers and then went to Cap'n Jack's, a burger place, to celebrate the victory. Jamila, Kristin, and I ended up in our own booth, and as soon as we were alone I leaned forward with my elbows on the table and said, "Guess what?"

Kristin was chugging a glass of water. "What?" Jamila asked, opening her menu.

"I met a guy," I announced.

Kristin put down her empty glass. "A guy? You're kidding! Who?"

"His name is Peter," I told them. "He has a nickname—Paco."

Kristin shook her head. "I don't think I know him. Is he a senior?"

"He doesn't go to South Regional," I said. "He works at Dave's."

Jamila's eyebrows drew together. "The gas station?"

"No, the jewelry store," I kidded. "Yeah, the gas station," I added in an anything-wrong-with-that? tone.

Kristin's eyes lit up. "The blond dreadlocks guy, right? He's *cute*."

"The blond dreadlocks guy? You're kidding! How did this happen?" Jamila wanted to know.

While we waited for our burgers and fries, I told them about the first time I'd bumped into Peter and the second time, including the party at Zeke's. "Did you kiss?" Kristin asked.

A giveaway blush stole up my face. "Sort of," I confessed.

"This is wild," Jamila said. "Straight-arrow Daisy and the funky guy from the gas station."

"I'm not a straight arrow," I protested.

Kristin laughed. "It's okay. We like you that way. And obviously Peter does, too."

The waitress had brought our food. "I would never have picked him for your type, though,"

Jamila admitted as she poured ketchup on her burger.

"He's different from anyone I've ever known," I agreed. "But that's what's cool about him. He's a nonconformist, and so are his friends. Getting good grades, being popular—they're not hung up on that stuff."

"Hmmm," said Kristin thoughtfully, munching a french fry.

"When are you going to see him again?" Jamila wondered.

"I don't know," I answered. I tried to sound casual, but inside, I had the same fluttery feeling I got every time I thought about Peter. Soon, I thought. I hope it's soon.

"You have to go already?" Rose said into the phone. "But it's only been five minutes!"

It was late Friday afternoon, and Rose was talking to Stephen. I was sitting at my desk, getting some books together to take to the hospital—I was working the six-to-ten shift.

"Well, okay. You can call me back tomorrow," Rose said. "I love you. Bye."

She hung up the phone, then folded her arms across her chest, scowling. "That was weird," she muttered.

"What?" I asked.

She turned to look at me. "Well, when I called Stephen last night, he was on his way to the library, you know? So he told me to call him today before dinner. And now he's on his way out the door again!"

"He's busy."

"Yeah, but doing what? There were all these voices in the background, like there were people in his room."

"He has two roommates," I reminded her.

"But there were *lots* of voices," Rose said. "Male *and* female."

"Stephen has friends," I concluded. "That's a crime?"

Rose sighed. "I'm being paranoid, aren't I?"

"Yep."

"I just feel so left out," she confessed. "Everything in his life is new and exciting. Meanwhile I'm getting more boring by the minute."

I had to laugh. Rose is anything but boring. "Right."

"But Daze, seriously," Rose said. "What if—"

Just then the telephone on the night table rang. Rose grabbed it. "Hello, Stephen?" Her hopeful smile faded. "Oh, sorry. Yes, just a second, she's right here," she said, handing the receiver to me.

"This is Daisy," I said.

"Daisy, it's Peter."

His voice was deep and a little bit raspy—it sent a shiver down my spine. "Hi," I squeaked. "What's up?"

"I was just thinking about the other night," Peter said. "I want to see you again."

His bluntness made me blush. "Oh, well, y-yeah," I stammered. "Umm . . . me too."

"Is tonight okay?"

"Tonight?" I repeated.

I glanced at Rose, who was walking toward the door. Turning back, she mouthed, "I'm leaving."

When the door shut behind her, I said to Peter, "Yes, tonight's okay. Why don't I meet you at Dave's?"

When I pulled into the gas station, I still couldn't believe I'd done it—called in sick at the hospital and then pretended to my family that I was heading off to my job. For an instant I *did* feel sick. What if Mom found out?

When Peter tossed his guitar in the back and then climbed into the passenger seat, though, I was glad I was there. I wanted something and I went for it, I thought, secretly pleased with myself.

"Where to?" I asked him.

"You're in the driver's seat," he pointed out. "You decide."

"Well . . . there's always good music at the Rusty Nail," I said. Rose goes there a lot with her friends. "Or we could get a pizza or see a movie."

"How about the beach?" Peter suggested.

"There's going to be a frost tonight. And I won't be able to handle the sand on crutches."

"Let's try it, anyway," he said, his eyes on my face. "The moonlight'll keep us warm."

The parking lot at the main town beach, south of Kettle Cove, was empty. We walked over to a bench with a view of the water. "In the summer the beach is so tame and touristy," Peter said. "Off-season, it gets wild again."

"Yeah," I agreed, my eyes on the black waves.

"Do you like storms?" he asked.

My father's fishing boat sank in a nor'easter. I shook my head. "No, I don't like storms."

"You like sunny weather." Peter took my hand and pulled me closer to him.

"I guess I do," I said softly.

"There's something I've wanted to do all week." He held both my hands now, his grip tight. "Kiss you."

I looked into his eyes, my own widening. "You do?"

His laugh was low and husky. "Don't you want me to?"

Suddenly my shyness disappeared. I answered him by leaning close, my face lifted to his.

The kiss was electrifying. I was glad I was sitting down—both my knees would have given out on me, the bad one *and* the good one. Peter had put both his arms around me, and mine had gone around him, and we were holding each other for the first time and it made my mind go blank.

We kissed again—less rushed, more thrilling. I hoped Peter couldn't tell that I hadn't done this much before. One thing was for sure, making out with Jay hadn't prepared me for how it would feel kissing Peter.

"You're not cold now, are you?" Peter asked when we drew apart a little.

I laughed breathlessly. "Hardly."

He slumped back on the bench, reaching for his guitar. "Yeah, if we heated up any more, we might melt." He started playing. "Listen, I worked some more on that song from the other day. Your song."

I closed my eyes and let the music wash over me.

"I like it," I told him when he finished. "I can't believe you wrote that yourself."

"I didn't actually *write* it," he said. "I don't read music—this isn't on paper anywhere. I just play for myself, you know? I don't care if anyone else listens. Unless it's you."

He put the guitar away. For a few minutes we sat side by side, looking out at the ocean. Then I turned to face him. Lifting a hand, I touched the hoop in his right earlobe. "I like this," I told him.

He gave me a crooked smile. "I'm getting another pierce next week—lost a bet with Amy. Will you like that, too?"

My cheeks felt warm in the frosty air. "Sure," I said.

Peter was looking at me with a funny expression in his eyes. "Wow, are you beautiful," he said at last.

I tucked my chin into my coat collar. "Uh, thanks."

"And sweet, too." He shook his head. "Man, it's just as well."

"What's just as well?"

"I was just thinking you'd be really hot if you loosened up a little," he said. "But maybe I couldn't handle it."

What was he saying? That I was a nerd? I didn't want him to think that. "I'm not totally wholesome," I told him.

He grinned. "I know. I could tell by that kiss.

But I mean *wild*, Daisy. Do you want to be wild?"

At that question a jumble of emotions ran through me. On the one hand, I was a little afraid. I'd spent my life playing by the rules. Could I even function without them? But as I stared into Peter's blue eyes I felt all the pressures I'd been under for so many months—for years even, ever since Dad died—fade away. The fear suddenly vanished. I was still in Hawk Harbor, but I felt as if I'd walked out of my life. I'd escaped.

Wild, I thought. Why shouldn't I be?

"Yes," I whispered to Peter as our lips met again.

Seven

"You're coming to the game at St. Joseph's today, right?" Jamila asked me at school on Thursday. The final bell had rung, and we were at our lockers. "I don't think so," I answered.

"You have to," Kristin urged. "You're our good luck mascot."

"Are you working?" Jamila guessed.

"Not today," I replied, sticking a textbook into my backpack.

"Well, if you're worried about the trig test, you could study on the bus," Kristin suggested. "I promise we won't bug you."

I was *not* worried about the trig test. "I'm seeing Peter," I told them.

"Wow," said Kristin. "You two have been spending a lot of time together."

"Yeah," I admitted. Peter and I had seen each other every day since our first real date the other night.

"When do we get to meet him?" Jamila asked.

I pictured clean-cut Kristin and Jamila hanging out with Peter's crowd. Kristin is allergic to cigarette smoke, and Jamila can't stand people who aren't in shape. Neither one of them drinks. "One of these days," I answered vaguely.

"Daze, I was talking to Mel during study hall, and she said you decided not to run for student council after all," Kristin said. "How come?"

I shrugged. "It just didn't seem like it was going to be cool. Every other junior running is a loser."

Kristin raised her eyebrows. "Matt Daly? Heather Holmes?"

Matt and Heather hung out with us sometimes. I shrugged again. "I guess I just didn't feel like it."

"You would have been great," Jamila said. "But it's your choice."

I turned to leave. "Good luck in the game."

"Thanks," Kristin said.

My friends seemed disappointed, but I didn't spend much time dwelling on that. I was too eager to get to Dave's Fuel 'n' Fix.

But when I hobbled outside, I found Peter waiting for me in front of the high school. "Hi!" I said, surprised.

He slipped an arm around my neck, pulling my face to his for a kiss. "Got my mom's car today," he said. "Come on."

When we were in his mother's old station wagon, I asked, "Don't you have to work today?"

"Nope. I quit."

"You *quit*? How come?"

"Dave. I'm telling you, that guy's a—" Peter broke off and slammed his palm against the steering wheel. "There was some money missing from the cash register last weekend, right? And he asked me about it in this way, like, forget about innocent until proven guilty, you know?"

I stared at Peter, confused. "You mean, Dave accused you of taking the money?"

"Not in so many words, but obviously he thinks it was me." Peter steered the Ford onto the street. "Supposedly someone had been rigging the receipts, like ringing up sales for a smaller amount and pocketing the extra cash, and he asked me did I know anything about it, and I just blew up, you know?"

"And you quit." I realized I sounded stupid, but I couldn't help it. I was stunned. I wasn't sure what part of the story was more upsetting—the fact that Peter had bagged his job or that his boss had accused him of stealing. I didn't have any experience with a situation like this. It threw me off balance.

"I'm not going to work for someone who doesn't trust me," Peter declared. "I don't need that kind of grief."

"Of course not," I said, suddenly feeling protective. I put a hand on Peter's arm and massaged his bicep. "Dave's a jerk."

"Hey, it's just a job." Peter punched the button on the radio, and the music started blasting. "I can find another one."

He was driving toward Kent—probably to the mall, where there's a movie theater and video arcade plus lots of cheap fast food. "I wonder who stole it?" I said. "If it wasn't you."

Peter yanked on the steering wheel, abruptly pulling over onto the shoulder. "It wasn't me, okay?" he insisted.

"I know it wasn't you," I said, but the way he'd snapped at me seemed strange. For a split second I had a terrible thought. What if Peter *did* steal the money? He was smart enough to figure out a way to do it without leaving behind any evidence.

I squashed the suspicion fast. Peter had dropped out of school, and he had kind of a cynical attitude, but that didn't mean he'd do something illegal. Society always trashes people like Peter. Caring about him meant loyalty, and that's something I'm good at. "I know it wasn't you," I repeated with conviction.

Peter looked into my eyes. "Thanks for believing in me, Daisy."

My family likes rituals: cutting down our own Christmas tree, having an egg hunt on Easter, the Fourth of July parade and fireworks in town, birthday parties. Every fall we go to McCloskey's Farm to pick apples and buy a pumpkin for Halloween. This year we went on a sunny Saturday afternoon in October. It was my first day without crutches—I limped along pretty slowly, but at least I was on both feet again.

Hal came along, too . . . unfortunately. "Let's pick some Northern Spies," Mom told him, pointing to the far side of the orchard. "They're the best for pies."

"Sure thing," said Hal, grabbing a bushel basket in one hand and taking Mom's hand with his other.

"Northern Spies for pies—hey, that rhymes. Ha, ha."

Laurel laughed, too, as if Hal had said something that was actually funny. Mom smiled at Hal in a sappy way. Plucking an apple from a tree as we walked by, Lily announced, "Mom, I want to get my ears pierced. At the Piercing Pavilion at the mall it only costs—"

"No," said Mom.

"But I have to have pierced ears," Lily informed her. "This is *important*, Mom."

"Let me guess." Hal winked at Mom. "Your friends at school have pierced ears."

"They do, Mr. Leverett, and they all have the same gold heart earrings, and—"

"You know the rule, Lily," Mom cut in. "When you're thirteen, you can have your ears pierced, but not before."

"But Mom!" wailed Lily, stamping her foot on the fallen leaves. "Without pierced ears I'll—"

"Next subject," Mom suggested, watching as Laurel hitched herself up onto a low branch to reach a couple of particularly big red apples. "What's happening at school for you these days, Laurel?"

I lifted my basket so Laurel could drop the apples into it. "Nothing much," she answered. "Oh, Nathan Green asked me to go out with him. I said yes," she added without much enthusiasm.

"That's nice," said Mom.

"Nathan's brother, Adam, was in my class," Rose reported. "If Nathan looks anything like him, he's a hunk."

"He's pretty cute," Laurel admitted with a melancholy sigh.

"Then why aren't you psyched?" Lily asked. "You are *so* strange."

"I don't know." Laurel jumped down from the tree, dusting off her hands on her jeans. "I thought maybe I should just do it—if everyone else is—have a boyfriend, I mean."

"Speaking of boyfriends," Rose said. "Daisy's been spending a lot of time with the mysterious Peter lately."

"That's right," said Mom.

"Yes, when are we going to meet this fellow?" asked Hal.

"I don't need your permission to date him," I snapped at Hal.

Everyone stopped walking and turned to stare at me. "I don't think that's what Hal meant, Daisy," Mom said, her forehead wrinkled.

"Sorry," I said, although I wasn't. "My mistake."

"We're just eager to meet your new friend, that's all," she went on. "Maybe you could invite him over for brunch or dinner tomorrow."

"Sure," I mumbled, kicking at a rotten windfall apple.

We wandered on through the orchard. Mom and Hal and Rose started gabbing about menu possibilities for a party Mom was catering in Portland the following weekend. Lily complained to Laurel about the injustice of not being allowed to have pierced ears; Laurel, tracking a family of pheasants through the underbrush, ignored her.

I trailed behind everyone else. My knee was killing me, and that wasn't all. I'd always enjoyed these outings, but not today. All at once apple picking seemed like a waste of time, and on top of that, my mom and my sisters and Hal most of all were getting on my nerves in a major way.

I picked a Macintosh apple and bit into it. "Yuck," I said, tossing it aside. "Worms."

So much for family rituals, I decided. From now on, count me out.

"You really want to have dinner with my family?" I asked Peter when we went out that night.

"Sure," he said. "What time should I be there?"

Dinnertime on Sunday rolled around, and I started to get nervous. I told myself to chill—it didn't really matter if Peter and my family hit it off. But when he rang the doorbell and I saw him standing there—wearing khakis and a pullover sweater like some prep from Seagate Academy—I couldn't help hoping. I was crazy about him, and I wanted Mom and Rose and Laurel and Lily to like him, too.

The evening started off pretty well, despite the fact that Hal was there as usual. Mom had made steak and twice-baked potatoes—she didn't go to that much trouble for just anybody. It means she's psyched about meeting Peter, I thought. And Peter's manners were great. "It's nice to meet you, Mrs. Walker," he said politely, shaking Mom's hand. He turned to Hal. "And you must be Mr. Leverett."

Hal shook Peter's hand, but I could see him checking out Peter's long hair and double-pierced ear.

We all sat down at the dining room table. Peter was across from me and next to Mom. "So, Peter," Mom said while Hal passed around the steak. "Are you in Daisy's class at school?"

I tensed up. Mom didn't know that Peter had dropped out . . . somehow I'd forgotten to mention it. Oh, God, she's going to freak, I thought.

"I'm not in school currently," Peter answered, not in the least bit thrown by the question. "I decided to take some time off from academics and acquire some real-world experience."

"Oh," said Mom. "Then you haven't graduated from high school yet?"

"I can always get my GED," Peter said offhandedly.

"I hope so," Mom said. "It's hard to have a career nowadays without a *college* degree, and I speak from experience."

"I'm not worried," he replied. "If I decide there's really a point in going back, I will. Right now I just don't see it."

Hal opened his mouth, probably to make a speech about the importance of education for people who want to have fascinating careers as accountants. Luckily Lily spoke up first. "I can't eat this, Mom," she said, pushing her plate away.

"Why not?" asked Mom.

"Because it's animal flesh," Lily explained. "Kendall, Kimberly, Talia, and Lindsey and me are on this vegan diet. That's strict vegetarian—no dairy, no eggs, no animal products at all, not even honey. It's really cleansing."

"I see," said Mom.

Rose laughed. "This will last about three hours, I bet," she predicted.

Lily frowned. "It will not. I'm committed."

"To giving up cheeseburgers and pizza and ice cream and Mom's chicken pie and lobster and fried clams?" Rose asked. "Have you ever actually *tasted* tofu, Lily?"

"Pass the carrots, please," Lily said, ignoring Rose.

Lily had provided a momentary distraction, but it didn't last. Mom put down her fork and turned back to Peter. "Since you're not a student right now, are you working, then, Peter?" she asked.

"I was working at Dave's Fuel 'n' Fix," he answered.

I prayed Mom wouldn't notice the past tense, but she doesn't miss a trick. "Was?"

"It didn't really turn me on," he told her. "Not enough intellectual stimulation. I mean, physical labor's cool, but I'd like to balance the brain and the body, you know?"

"Are you looking for another job?" she asked.

Peter nudged my foot under the table and smiled at me. I happened to know he was just hanging out. "Yeah, I'm polishing up my resume," he said.

I shot a desperate, please-change-the-subject glance at Rose.

"Did I tell you guys about the acting class I'm going to take next semester at the community college?" she asked brightly.

The rest of the meal went okay once Mom and Hal stopped grilling Peter. I only managed to eat a few bites, though. Not because I'm becoming a vegetarian like Lily but because my stomach had tied itself into an anxious knot. I know my mom really well, and even though she was smiling, I could tell she wasn't all that thrilled by Peter. I don't care what she thinks, I told myself. I don't care what any of them think! But if that was true, how come I felt like crying?

When Peter was ready to go, I walked him out to the street. "I think that went okay," he said, putting his arms around me as we stood on the sidewalk near his car.

"Yeah," I lied.

"Your family's not bad. A little uptight, but I've seen worse. And your sisters are babes."

He tickled my waist a little, and I snuggled close for a kiss. "When will I meet *your* family?" I asked. "Your mom and aunt Trish?"

"No rush," Peter said. "I did this for you tonight, but in general I'm not into the meeting-the-family routine. I don't have anything to say to Mom and Aunt Trish, you know? Just because we share the same genetic material doesn't mean we click."

"Oh," I said. "Right." I've always thought family was really important, but maybe Peter had a point. Being related didn't necessarily mean you got along. "See you tomorrow?" I asked.

"Absolutely," he replied.

"Love you," I said. I caught my breath a little as the words left my lips. I hadn't said them to him before. Please let him say it back, I thought. Please let him feel the same way I do.

Peter smiled and then he kissed me again. "Love you, too, Sleeping Beauty."

"So, what did you think of Peter?" I asked Rose later after Peter had left and she and I were alone in our room, listening to music and doing homework. I was still flying from telling Peter I loved him.

Rose turned her desk chair to face me, flipping her long hair back over her shoulder. "You really want to know?"

Now I regretted asking the question, but it was already out there. "Sure."

"Well, he seems bright. And he's cute," Rose said. "But . . ."

"But what?"

"Don't take this the wrong way, okay?" she advised. "But he's not in school, he doesn't do sports or anything like that. He's not ambitious the way you are. Are you sure he's the right boy for you?"

"So what if he's not going to Harvard like Stephen?" I countered angrily. "Maybe if he'd had Stephen's advantages, he'd be on that track, but his life's been really hard."

"I didn't say he had to go to Harvard," Rose replied. "Look, you asked my opinion. I just think you haven't dated that much, and maybe you don't know what you're looking—"

"I love Peter and he loves me and that's all there is to it," I declared.

Rose's eyes widened. "Well, okay. If that's how it is, Daze, you know I just want you to be—"

I interrupted her again. "Maybe Peter's not perfect, but neither am I. And I'm not going to break up with him just because you and Mom and Hal don't approve of him. Unlike some people in this family, I believe in loyalty."

Rose frowned. "What's *that* supposed to mean?"

"Who was that guy on the phone before?"

"You mean Craig? He's in my economics class."

"That's not the first time he's called."

"And your point is?"

"You already have a boyfriend."

"Sure, but that doesn't mean I can't make new friends," Rose said.

"I just think people should be faithful to each other," I argued.

Rose looked at me for a moment and then glanced at the picture of Dad on my night table. "Are you talking about me or about Mom?" she asked quietly.

I shook my head, confused. I didn't know *who* I was talking about or what. I just knew that tonight my knee hurt like crazy, and the pain had spread through my whole body and settled in my heart. I just knew that for whatever reason, the only thing that made me feel better anymore was being with Peter.

Eight

"Finally we get to party with Peter!" Jamila said.

It was Friday night, and Jamila had invited a bunch of people over to her house. We were in the basement, listening to music and playing silly games like Ping-Pong with five people on a side. "That is, if he ever shows up," she added.

"He'll show up," I promised. Kristin, Jamila, and I were lounging on beanbag chairs, within arm's reach of a giant bowl of Cheez Doodles. "He wanted to meet me here because he has a job interview at the video store at the mall tonight."

"That's cool," Kristin remarked.

"Yeah, I hope he gets it," I said. It had seemed a *little* weird lately with Peter not in school and not working, either. Not that I would ever criticize him—I wouldn't want to sound like somebody's parent. I respected the fact that he needed time to figure out what he wanted to do with his life. "First crack at the new releases, you know?"

Just then Jamila waved to someone coming down the stairs. "Speak of the devil," said Kristin.

"Hi!" I called.

Peter crossed the room to join us. He was wearing

seriously baggy jeans and a ripped T-shirt. Nice outfit for a job interview, I couldn't help thinking. His long blond hair was pulled back in a ponytail, so when he leaned in to kiss me, I noticed his gothic-style crucifix earring and also a new gold stud in his left ear. "Hey, you got pierced again," I said.

"The interview stunk, so I went over to the Piercing Pavilion to say hi to Alison, and the next thing I knew, bang." Peter grinned. "She got me with the gun."

"Peter's friend Alison works at the Piercing Pavilion," I explained to Jamila and Kristin. "For that reason Lily thinks he's a god."

"So, the interview at the video store didn't go well?" Kristin asked.

"The guy was a total jerk," Peter answered. "Making this big deal about checking my references, you know?"

"They always do that," Jamila pointed out.

"Yeah, well, I wasn't about to give him Dave's number. What, so he could call the gas station and hear about stuff I didn't even do? I just told the guy, 'Later.'"

I slipped my arm around Peter and gave him a supportive squeeze. "Too bad the guy was a jerk," I said.

Kristin and Jamila exchanged a glance. "Yeah, too bad," Kristin said.

"I think it's Twister time," Jamila announced, getting to her feet. "Want to play?"

Peter cocked one eyebrow. "Twister? You mean, that lame 'left hand on red' game?"

"It's fun," Kristin said.

"I'll pass," Peter said.

Jamila nudged me. "What about you, Daisy?"

"Um, you know, my knee's bothering me a little. I'll just hang out with Peter."

We watched Jamila and Kristin round up Phil, Raj, and Molly. In a couple of minutes bodies were tangled up all over the place. Smiling, I looked at Peter. He was yawning. "So, where's the beer?" he asked.

I couldn't tell if he was kidding or not. "My friends don't drink. Want a soda?"

"We could be at a rave in Portland—Amy and Marcus were going," Peter told me.

"A rave?"

"A *real* party."

"If you're not having fun, we can leave," I said.

"Hey, no. This is cool." Peter hugged me. "Whatever."

We didn't stay much longer, though. Peter didn't feel like talking to my friends or playing Ping-Pong, and because of my knee we couldn't dance. We ended up back at his aunt's ranch house, which is about a mile from where I live, making out on the living room couch.

"You're sure this is okay?" I whispered, wriggling away from him slightly.

"Aunt Trish is out, and Mom's asleep," Peter assured me, locking his arms around my body and pulling me close again. "She takes a ton of meds plus sleeping pills. We'd have to bang cymbals next to her ears to wake her up."

We kissed again, and I started to get a little worried. Peter had more experience with sex than I did, and I knew he wanted us to sleep together, but I wasn't even close to being ready for that. I was relieved when he got up, saying, "Want a drink? I know where my aunt keeps the good stuff." Crossing the room, he opened a cabinet. "Bourbon, scotch, vodka. Name your poison."

I sat up, gingerly flexing my sore knee. "No, thanks."

He faced me, a bottle in his hand. "One of these days you should give it a try. Good things would happen."

I shrugged. "I just don't feel like I need it."

He put the bottle back in the cupboard. "Okay, we'll do it your way." Smiling, he came over and pinned me back on the couch. "Stone-cold sober."

We kissed pretty intensely, but it was hard for me to relax. I decided I'd better distract him before things got too steamy. "Thanks for going to Jamila's party with me," I said.

"No problem."

"Did you have fun?"

"It was okay."

Just okay? I thought. Couldn't he lie to make me feel better? My disappointment only lasted an instant, though. Of course Peter wouldn't lie—that was what I liked about him, that he didn't feel like he had to impress people. He was just himself, take it or leave it.

Peter was still holding me, and now his arms tightened. "Forget the party. All I wanted all night was to be alone with you. I love you so much, Daisy."

"I love you, too," I said as our lips met in a passionate kiss. And I did. Maybe Peter didn't get along so great with my friends or with my family. Did that matter? I don't get along all that well with my family these days, either, I thought. If I had to make a choice, Peter was it.

It did end up turning into a choice. I wanted to spend time with Peter, so that meant I didn't have time for a lot of other things. I kept my job at the hospital because I needed the money, but I stopped going to watch my friends play soccer, and I blew off chores and homework. When my first-quarter report card came, it was a shock. "Two C's and only one A-minus," I told Peter as we sat in the Ice Cream Shoppe one afternoon in early November, eating hot fudge sundaes. "I've never gotten a C in my life. Mom's going to kill me!"

"Grades are meaningless," Peter declared. "Just some screwed-up teacher's subjective evaluation. Why should you let other people's expectations rule your life?"

I nodded. "You're right. A report card's just a stupid piece of paper. I'm not even going to show it to Mom."

Peter's aunt was working, and his mom was at the doctor's in Portland, so we spent the rest of the afternoon at his house watching soaps. He has a whole lineup that he watches since he's not working. I tried to get him to switch to the public television station—an interesting documentary about

Thomas Jefferson—but he thought it was boring.

When I got home, it was dinnertime. It had been ages since I'd helped cook or set the table or anything like that, and as I came into the kitchen Mom started to lecture me, but when she saw me, the words died on her lips. "Daisy, I wish you'd come home in time to—" Her mouth dropped open. "What did you *do* to your hair?"

"Oh, my God," exclaimed Rose, almost dropping the salad bowl she was holding. "It's worse than that time in eighth grade!"

Peter and I had been bored, so he'd given me a buzz cut with an electric razor. Then I'd dyed what was left of my blond hair jet black. "You are *so* conservative," I said to Rose, my tone disdainful.

Just then Lily entered the room. "Wow, look at Daisy," she said admiringly. "Man, are you *ugly.*"

Mom glanced at Lily. "That's not very nice," she said. "I guess if Daisy wants—wait a minute." Mom narrowed her eyes. "Lily. Your *ears!*"

Lily took a step backward, as if she thought Mom was going to rip the gold studs from her earlobes. "I went to the Piercing Pavilion," she said in a rush, "and Peter's friend Alison did it for free!"

Mom turned back to me. "Did you know Lily was getting her ears pierced?" she asked.

"I didn't have anything to do with it," I said, which was true. "But what's the big deal, anyway?"

"The big deal is that I told her she had to wait until she was thirteen," Mom snapped. "And I—"

The buzzer on the stove went off. Mom shook

her head, exasperated. "The casserole's ready. We might as well eat while it's hot. But I'll talk to you after dinner, young lady," she told Lily.

When dinner was over, though, Lily escaped discipline. Mom was picking on me again. "I've seen everyone else's report card," she said. "Where's yours, Daisy?"

"I think I left it in my locker," I mumbled.

"You think?"

It was still hard for me to lie to her. "Well, maybe I have it," I admitted, and walked over to the foot of the stairs, where I'd tossed my backpack. I pulled out the crumpled report card. "Here," I said defiantly, handing it to Mom.

She scanned the grades and then looked up at me. I braced myself. "Daisy, I'm . . . ," she began.

"Mad?" My tone was belligerent. "Disappointed?"

"No, I'm . . . worried. Daisy, since you met Peter, you—"

"It doesn't have anything to do with Peter," I cut in. "Those are my grades, not his."

"I know." Mom's gaze took in my haircut and the midriff T-shirt and baggy black jeans I'd just bought at the mall. "But you've had such a great academic record until now. Grades are important. When you apply to colleges next year—"

"I'll worry about next year next year," I interrupted.

"I'd appreciate being allowed to finish my sentences," Mom said sternly.

"Sorry. Please go on," I said with elaborate politeness. "I'm listening."

She frowned. "This fresh attitude is another thing I'm not too happy about."

"Look, are we done with this conversation? Because maybe I should work on my homework, right, Mom?"

"We're not quite done," she said. "One more strike and you're out, Daisy. Grounded. Do I make myself clear?"

"You're *punishing* me because you don't like my *attitude?*" I asked in disbelief.

Mom stared back at me without blinking. "If you keep performing poorly at school and missing curfew, yes, I'll punish you."

I turned away and walked upstairs without responding.

Rose had gone to a night class at the community college, so I had the bedroom all to myself. Unbelievable. Absolutely unbelievable, I thought as I walked past the mirror on my way to pick up the phone to call Peter and tell him Mom had ragged on me about the report card.

Then I stopped, surprised by my own reflection. I looked wild with my short black hair and outrageous clothes. For a split second I wondered, Who is that girl?

I smiled grimly at myself. Mom thought Peter was a bad influence on me—so what if he was? "It's my choice," I whispered to my reflection. I'd always, always done the right thing my whole life, and who'd ever appreciated it? Not Mom.

Why shouldn't I do the *wrong* thing for once?

*   *   *

"You're doing a terrific job," Jody told me a couple of nights later. "Do you like the work?"

She pulled up a chair to sit next to me at the reception desk. "Sure," I said. "Hospitals are interesting."

"I'm worried that you're getting bored," Jody said. "How would you like to take on some other responsibilities?"

"Like what?"

"We need someone to organize social activities for the kids on the ward, like our Thanksgiving dinner in a couple of weeks, and to help coordinate volunteers. It would mean working more closely with patients *and* with doctors and nurses."

"Oh. Um . . ." I thought about it. I kind of liked the reception desk; it kept me at a comfortable distance from what was actually going on in the hospital. Do I *want* to get closer? I wondered. "I'm not sure, Jody."

"Well, we can talk about it some more." She patted my arm, then stood up. "Hey, Ben," she said.

I turned. "Hey, Jody," Ben said. He came up and took the seat Jody had just vacated, pulling his chair right next to mine. Talk about close, I thought. More like in your face!

"Are you trying to look like me?" he joked, pointing to my cropped hair.

"Yeah, maybe I *should* just shave it all off."

For a second he didn't say anything. "Who are you mad at?" he asked finally.

I was taken aback. "What do you mean?"

"Cutting your hair."

"I'm not mad at anybody," I told him. "I just wanted a change."

Ben was wearing a bathrobe, and he had a blanket wrapped around him as well. He's so thin, he gets cold easily. Now he pulled the edge of the blanket up over his head like a hood. "I bet your mom loves it."

"As a matter of fact, she hates it," I said. "She hates everything about me lately." I told him about our most recent blowup. "I have to get my grades back up or else."

"Well, yeah, of course," Ben commented. "What's she supposed to say, 'It's okay with me if you slack off and throw away your future'?"

"It was just a report card," I protested.

"Right. Grades are meaningless." I cringed. He couldn't know that he was echoing Peter. Of course, the difference was that Ben was being sarcastic. "They just go on your permanent transcript, which goes to the colleges you apply to, who decide whether you get in or not, which determines the rest of your life, basically." He shrugged under the blanket. "No biggie."

He stood up. "Where are you going?" I asked, wondering why it didn't tick me off when Ben lectured me.

"To my room to study. Ciao."

I watched Ben make his way slowly down the corridor. I couldn't believe he was still trying to keep up with his classes. He'd missed so much school, I'd assumed he would have to repeat the year. Or would he? People could do almost anything when they want it badly enough, and Ben wanted it. I used to be the same way, I thought. Not anymore.

On Thanksgiving morning Mom had gotten up early to stuff the turkey. The bird was already in the oven and she was having a cup of coffee with Rose when I came into the kitchen. "Good morning," Rose called from the table as I poured a bowl of cereal.

"Morning," I replied sleepily.

"You and Peter were out late last night," Mom commented.

Oh no. Here it comes, I thought. "Hmmm," I mumbled.

"Past curfew," Mom went on. "We talked about this the other night, Daisy."

"We did," I agreed, pulling a jug of milk from the fridge.

"Look at me, Daisy," Mom requested.

I looked at her, one eyebrow lifted so she wouldn't think I was intimidated.

"It was just a few minutes last night, so I'll give you one more chance, but that's all," she warned.

"You just don't like Peter," I accused. "Why don't you admit it?"

"I'm simply talking about the rules of this house," she replied. "They apply to all of you equally, and if you want to be part of this family, you can start following them."

I looked at Rose, who was eating cantaloupe at the table. She just shrugged. "Whatever," I said, opting for one of Peter's favorite expressions.

Around noon I was reading a magazine on my bed when Rose came to find me. "We're making the pies," she announced.

"So?"

"So, you always slice the apples while I make the crust," she reminded me.

"Laurel can slice the apples."

"Not as well as you. Come on."

"I'm comfortable here," I told her.

Rose put her hands on her hips. "It's *Thanksgiving*, Daze," she said. "Can't you snap out of it for once?"

"Look, I don't feel like it, okay?"

Rose looked like she was going to keep arguing. Then she shook her head. "Okay, have it your way," she grumbled as she stomped off. "See if I care."

For an instant I thought about running after Rose. Laurel would probably make a mess of the apples. Halfway off the bed, though, a twinge in my bad knee made me wince. Flopping back down, I picked up the magazine again. Who needed corny pie-baking rituals, anyway?

And here's something else I don't need, I thought an hour later as my family gathered around the dining room table. Hal, the master turkey carver. I couldn't believe I'd been naive enough to think we could have a meal without him.

"I don't think I'm hungry," I announced, staying on my feet while everyone else pulled out chairs and sat down.

"Don't you feel well?" Mom asked.

"No, I'm just not . . ." I stuck my hands in the pockets of my jeans. I hadn't bothered to put on a dress like my sisters. "I think I'll go over to Peter's."

Out of the corner of my eye I saw Hal frown. "Are they having Thanksgiving dinner over there?" Rose asked.

"No. His mom and aunt went to some relative's house. Peter's just hanging out." I headed for the door. "I'll see you later."

"This is a family occasion, Daisy," Hal spoke up. "I think you'd better—"

"Let her go," Mom said. "It's her choice."

I'd been ready to talk back to Hal, but the way Mom sounded more sad than mad made me feel like a jerk. I kept going, though, because I'd made up my mind to do it and because I really *wasn't* hungry. My sisters watched me, different expressions on each of their faces: Rose looked serious, Laurel looked puzzled, and Lily looked amazed and impressed that I hadn't gotten in more trouble. None of them understands, I thought as I grabbed a coat from the hall closet. The door to the apartment banged shut behind me. They just didn't get it.

For a minute I stood on the sidewalk, looking up and down Main Street. Because of the holiday Hawk Harbor was even deader than usual. The sun was out, but it was cold. It was starting to feel like winter.

Since it was only a mile, I decided to walk to Peter's. My knee would be killing me by the time I got there, but maybe the exercise would be good for it—and Mom would be *really* ticked if I took the car without asking. Not that I care what she thinks, I reminded myself.

As I walked along, though, past stores and restaurants closed for Thanksgiving or for the season I started to feel more and more bummed. I tried to push away the thoughts and memories of past Thanksgivings with my family. With Dad. Peter is all I need, I told myself. I hoped it was true.

Nine

The week after Thanksgiving, Coach Wheeler called me to his office. I hadn't talked to him in a month, and I felt self-conscious as I knocked on his door. He's going to laugh at my hair, I thought, suddenly wishing it was still long and blond.

He didn't laugh at my hair, although he gave me a pretty good look-over. "Sit down, Daisy."

I perched on the edge of the beat-up chair across from his desk, not getting comfortable because I didn't plan to stay long. "What's up?"

"We missed you at the tournament," he said.

The girls' soccer team had made it to the county play-offs. "How'd you do?" I asked.

"You should've seen the semifinal game against the Tigers. The girls played their hearts out. We lost in overtime, but it was close."

My eyes wandered over to the door. I really wanted to get out of there. Was he trying to make me feel guilty? "There's always next year," I mumbled.

Coach Wheeler leaned forward, his elbows on his desk. "Come to the sports banquet on Saturday night," he urged. "Your name is on the tournament plaque—I'll have a varsity certificate for you."

I looked at him, my expression bitter. I hated being reminded of the season I'd lost. "I didn't earn it."

"Sure, you did. You're still part of the team, Daisy."

I shrugged, looking away again. A minute passed. Then Coach Wheeler said, "So, what have you been up to lately?"

"Not much," I replied. "Just kind of hanging out."

"How's the knee coming along?"

"Okay. Um, Coach." I stood up. "If it's all right, I've got to run. Study hall's almost over, and I still need to finish my math."

"Right." He stood up, too. "I just wanted to check in with you since it's been a while. Stay in touch, Daiserooni."

Now, instead of feeling bitter, I suddenly felt sad. The silly nickname reminded me of so many great times, and his tone had remained affectionate and fatherly despite my foul attitude. I don't know why I'd never realized before that he cared about me.

I nodded, not meeting his eyes. "Sure."

He walked me to the door. For a second I thought he was going to hug me, but instead he just gave me this little good-bye salute. Which is just as well because if he'd put a hand on my shoulder or something, I might have started to cry.

It must have been national Check In with Daisy Day because right after the last bell, Kristin and Jamila ambushed me at my locker. "Hey, Daisy," said Jamila. "Can you believe it? We're free women—soccer's over for the year."

"How does it feel?" I asked.

"Great," answered Kristin. "Like getting out of prison."

Jamila laughed. "It wasn't *that* bad, but it's cool having afternoons off. We're thinking about catching a five o'clock movie at the mall. Want to come?"

"I don't know," I said.

"Oh, come on," Kristin urged. "We never see you anymore!"

She didn't sound critical, but I felt guilty, anyway. It must have shown on my face because Jamila jumped in quickly. "Hey, it's okay. We're your buds—we know how it is, a serious boyfriend and all that. We just miss you, Daze."

I looked at my friends, not sure how I was feeling, whether I missed them or not. "A movie would be fun, but I'm pretty sure Peter's expecting me to stop by," I said. "Maybe some other time, okay?"

Kristin and Jamila exchanged a glance. Then Jamila smiled, but she looked sad. "Sure, Daze. Some other time."

They walked off, and I stood by my locker for another minute. I thought about calling after them, but I didn't. What would I say? They don't know me anymore, I realized. We've grown apart. Why? Was I out of the loop because I'd stopped playing sports with them? Was it because I could tell they weren't crazy about Peter? And Coach Wheeler, I thought. I used to really open up to him, but just now in his office even if I'd wanted to . . .

I slammed my locker shut. My old friends were

worried about me. They thought I'd changed, and they wanted to know what was going on with me. And I can't tell them, I thought as I headed out to the line of school buses, because I don't know.

On Saturday morning I stayed in bed until eleven. I never used to sleep in, but lately I'd been having a hard time getting started in the morning. This morning was worse than usual because I'd stayed up later than usual the night before. I'd gotten in past my curfew by a measly five minutes because Peter and I had to fix a flat tire on his car. Mom had been waiting up for me, and she'd had no mercy. I was officially grounded for the first time in my life: No going out with Peter or anyone for two whole weeks.

I was thinking about getting out of bed when I heard Rose and Laurel's voices out in the hall. "Should we see if Daisy wants to go?" Laurel asked Rose.

I sat up to listen. "Are you kidding?" Rose responded. "She never wants to do anything these days. It wouldn't fit her *image*, you know?"

Their voices receded. Where are they going? I wondered. A minute later someone rapped on my door. "Come in," I said, expecting one of my sisters.

The door swung open. Mom took a step into my room. "We're going to McCloskey's to cut down a tree," she announced, her manner stiff.

"Is that an invitation? I thought I was grounded," I replied.

"We can wait while you get dressed," Mom offered. "If you want to come."

"Don't bother. I might as well get used to being imprisoned."

Mom looked like she was about to say something else, but she didn't. She left, closing the door quietly behind her.

I sat on my bed for a few more minutes. When I heard the front door to the apartment slam, I limped into the hall—my knee is always stiff in the morning.

The apartment was quiet. "Anybody home?" I called. No one answered.

I went to the front window and leaned on the sill. Looking down at the street, I could see my family piling into the car. Hal was there, too. Before he got in the passenger seat—Mom was driving—he tossed a length of rope and a handsaw in the trunk.

Watching them, I had a pang for the old days. Cutting down a Christmas tree is a family tradition. When we lived on Lighthouse Road, we'd always picked one from our own woods. We'd do it at the beginning of December so we could enjoy it all month long.

The car drove off, and I turned away from the window. I was alone.

That afternoon I had to answer phones at the hospital from two until six. Ben showed up before I'd even taken off my coat. "Hi," I said, sticking my book bag under the reception desk. "I thought you'd be at home by now."

"They're keeping me another week," he replied. "I'm on this new protocol, and they want to do some more radiation treatments. What's new?"

I dropped into my chair and glanced at the list of which doctors were on call. "I'm grounded for missing curfew. I can go to school and come here, but no parties or dates for two weeks. Can you believe it?"

"Uh . . . yeah. Your mom said she'd ground you, didn't she?" Ben reminded me. "You've got to respect her for sticking to her guns."

I hadn't looked at it that way, not that looking at it that way helped much. "I still think it's unfair," I said. "Has *your* mom ever grounded you?"

Ben laughed. "Are you kidding? I have *cancer.* She lets me do whatever I want."

I laughed, too. "That makes sense."

"I could get away with murder if I wanted to. But I don't want to waste my time testing limits."

"I'm not testing any limits," I said. "I'm just trying to live my life. And now I have no life."

"Well, here's a project for you," he said. "Help with the holiday party on the kids' ward. I'm going to be Santa."

I had to laugh. Ben weighs about a hundred pounds. "You?"

He grinned. "So I'll need major padding. Will you?"

"What?"

"Help."

I pointed to my spiky black hair. "I don't know. I'd make a pretty scary elf."

"None of us is winning any beauty contests these days," Ben reminded me.

I shook my head. "It wouldn't be my thing. Why are *you* doing it, anyway?"

"You mean, why put on a stupid Santa suit and act like there's a reason to be jolly when we're all sick and some of us will probably die?"

"That's not what I meant," I protested softly, although it was, sort of.

Ben gets tired really easily. Now he pulled up a chair and slumped forward with his arms folded on the desk, his chin propped on one hand. His eyes stayed on mine, though, and his gaze was intense. "Well, what's the alternative?" he asked. "I got dealt a rotten hand with this brain tumor. So what? I should just roll over and die? Just give up on myself . . . and those other kids?"

I stared at Ben. For some reason I thought about Peter. Hadn't he said something like that once, about getting a bad deal? I tried to picture my boyfriend dressing up as Santa Claus for a bunch of sick children but couldn't. He'd think it was so lame, I thought.

"Maybe you're right," Ben said, and he looked like he was about to cry.

"No," I said quietly. I put out my hand and touched his. "No, Ben, I'm not right. *You* are."

Peter picked me up in his aunt's car at eight. Mom had given me a night off from being grounded to go to the sports banquet. Marcus and Amy were already in the backseat. "Paco told us you're blowing off some sports banquet," Amy remarked as I climbed into the car. "Smart."

Jamila and Kristin had both tried to talk me into going, but at the last minute I'd decided to go out with Peter instead. "I didn't even finish the season," I said, buckling my seat belt.

"Just a bunch of dumb jocks, anyway," Marcus commented. "Talk about boring, right?"

Those "dumb jocks" were some of my closest friends, or they had been, anyway, but I didn't say so. "Where are we going?" I asked Peter as he hit the gas.

He shot me a glance, smiling mischievously. "Are you in the mood for some fun?"

"Sure," I said. Marcus and Amy both laughed. "I guess," I added, wondering what the joke was.

Marcus and Amy laughed again, and so did Peter. Then Peter cranked the radio, thumping out the beat on the steering wheel with his hands and rocking in his seat as he drove. "Where are we going?" I asked again.

"You'll see," he said, grinning at Marcus and Amy in the rearview mirror.

Five minutes later he pulled into the parking lot of the Liquor Locker on the Old Boston Post Road. I turned to Peter. "They won't sell to us," I said.

"Just watch a couple of experts at work," Peter advised.

He and Marcus got out of the car and strode into the liquor store. Amy crawled into the driver's seat. "They are so cool," she said.

We watched the guys through the store window. Peter had wandered out of sight. Marcus was at the cash register, talking to the clerk. Marcus must have cracked a joke. The clerk laughed. Then Marcus pointed, and the clerk turned to look at the shelf behind him.

That's when Peter reappeared . . . walking straight toward the door with a case of beer tucked under his arm, as calm as if he did this sort of thing every day of his life.

Amy started the engine, and Peter jumped into the backseat. When Marcus had hopped in, too, Amy peeled out of the parking lot. The three of them were laughing so hard, I thought Amy was going to drive off the road. For a minute I was too shocked to speak. Then Amy said, "Where do you want to party, Paco?"

"You need to take me home," I blurted suddenly.

Peter leaned forward, his hands gripping my shoulders. "But the party's just getting started."

"I feel sick," I said, and it was true. "I think I'm going to throw up or something."

"You'll feel better after a beer or two," Peter promised, massaging my shoulders.

"I don't think so," I said.

"Give it a try."

"Could you just take me home, please?"

Amy looked at Peter for guidance. He nodded.

When we got to my building, Peter walked me to the door. "You're sure you don't want to go out?" he asked.

I shook my head. "I probably just need a good night's sleep." I thought about leaving it at that, but I would have hated myself for being such a wimp. Underage drinking was one thing; petty theft was another. "Peter, did you have to do that? Steal the beer?"

He laughed. "It's just a case of cheap stuff. It won't hurt their profit margins."

Suddenly I recalled the gas station theft. Had that been Peter after all? "Maybe not, but if everybody took whatever they felt like—"

Peter struck his forehead with the palm of his hand, speaking to the sky. "I'm trying to impress the girl, and she reads me the riot act!"

I stared at him. This baffled me more than anything else that had happened tonight. Didn't Peter know me at all? "You thought that would *impress* me?"

"I thought we could have a good time, that's all," he said. He kissed me on the lips. "I'll talk to you tomorrow."

I kissed him back and then ducked into the building. In our apartment I went straight to my room so no one could ask me any questions. For a long time I lay on my bed in the dark, too wired to close my eyes. I thought about Peter and the liquor store, Jamila and Kristin at the sports banquet, my knee injury, Ben Compton's cancer, Mom and Hal, Dad. Nothing seemed to fit anymore or to make sense. I was mad at Peter for stealing the beer . . . or was I mad at myself? Am I just too uptight? I wondered. So what if Peter wanted to get trashed with his friends?

That wasn't all there was to it, though, and I knew it. It wasn't about having fun—it was about right and wrong. Was it possible that Peter genuinely didn't know the difference?

Since I loved him, should I try to teach him? Would he even let me?

It was hours later when I finally fell asleep.

Ten

"Merry Christmas, Daisy!" Lily yelled into the bedroom.

I glanced at the clock on my night table and then rolled over, burying my face in my pillow. My family had gone to Christmas Eve services at church the night before, and I'd gone out with Peter. I wasn't grounded anymore, but Mom was still breathing down my neck and being totally judgmental about everything I did. I had a new, ridiculously early curfew that Peter and I had gotten around by coming back to my house and watching videos on the family room couch until three in the morning.

Now it was Laurel's turn to shout. "Get out of bed, Daze, or we're going to start opening presents without you!"

"I'm coming, I'm coming," I mumbled.

I put a sweatshirt on over my pajamas and stuck my feet in some slippers. Shuffling downstairs, I joined everybody around the tree. Mom was sipping coffee; Rose was loading film in her camera; Lily and Laurel were on hands and knees, checking out the packages under the tree. "Wow, here's a big one for you, Daze," Lily announced.

"Yeah?" I said, surprised. I hadn't expected much—I hadn't been too "good" lately.

"Can we start opening, Mom?" Laurel asked eagerly.

Mom gave Laurel the green light, and the wrapping paper began to fly. Christmas has gotten simpler in our family since Dad died. To save money, there are a lot of homemade presents, and it's a tradition to give each other favors, like making your sister's bed for a week—stuff like that. The holiday still means a lot, though, and as I saw Lily and Laurel's bright eyes and smiles as they opened their presents, I felt guilty that I hadn't put more thought into my gifts. I'd tried to get Peter to go Christmas shopping at the mall with me, but he refused and went on some tirade about "commercialism," so I'd just bought a few bottles of bubble bath at the drugstore in town. "Yum, this smells good," said Rose when she opened her bubble bath.

"Big deal, huh?" I mumbled.

"I like it," she assured me. "I can't wait to take a bath tonight."

"You'll smell pretty for Stephen," Lily said.

Rose frowned. "For what it's worth—he's going back to school the day after tomorrow."

"Isn't he on vacation?" Laurel asked.

"Yes, but he says he has some independent study project he's working on." Rose bit her lip. "I can't help thinking there must be some other reason. . . . Anyway." She forced a smile. "Who's next?"

"Speaking of smelling pretty," said Mom, "whose perfume is in the air?"

Laurel, sitting next to Mom, blushed slightly. "It's me," she admitted. "'Windswept.' Nathan gave it to me for Christmas."

"How *romantic*," teased Rose.

Laurel rolled her eyes. "Yeah."

At that moment the doorbell rang. Lily ran to get it. When she came back into the living room, Laurel's friend Jack Harrison was with her, wearing a blue blazer and tie under his parka. "Merry Christmas," he greeted us.

Laurel's face was now as red as Santa's suit. "What are *you* doing here?" she asked, none too graciously.

"We're on our way down to Boston for Christmas dinner with my cousins," he explained, "and my parents had something for you." He handed Mom a basket of fruit tied with a big green velvet bow.

Mom kissed Jack on the cheek. "Take this down to them," she said, giving him a tin of homemade Christmas cookies, "and tell them we'll see them at the New Year's Eve party."

Mr. and Mrs. Harrison were parked on the street below, but Jack didn't seem in a huge hurry to leave. "Are you and Nathan coming to the party?" he asked Laurel politely.

Jack's parents give a big New Year's Eve party every year, and they invite everybody—grown-ups and kids. "I don't know," Laurel said.

Jack put a hand to his tie. "Tammy gave me this," he reported. "Her mom helped her pick it out."

Laurel eyed the tie with distaste. "Great."

"Well, have a fun day," Jack said.

"Come by again soon, Jack," Mom told him.

When Jack was gone, Lily declared, "Well, it's obvious he's still into you, although who knows why."

"Let's get back to presents," said Rose. She handed me the large package Lily had noticed before.

I read the tag. "It's from all of you," I said. "What is it?"

"Open it and find out," Laurel suggested.

I tore off the paper. Inside was a box. "Richardson's Sports," I said. "A softball glove!"

"I bumped into Larry Wheeler in town last week," Rose explained, "and we were talking about spring and how you'd probably be ready to play, and I thought—"

"No, it was my idea," Lily cut in. "Your old one is so beat up, and I talked to the guy at the store and he said this was the best glove they carry and—"

Laurel cut to the chase. "Do you like it?"

I stared down at the new glove. I hadn't done anything athletic in months. It was so hard to imagine running and throwing and sliding again. "I don't know if I'll play softball in the spring, but . . . yeah, sure. It's a great glove. Thanks."

Rose said, "You could always trade it for something else like . . ."

"A tennis racket," said Lily.

"Golf clubs!" said Laurel.

Everyone laughed. I cracked a smile, too, despite myself. "Right, and which package has the country club membership?" I joked.

*   *   *

I thought about blowing off Christmas dinner the way I did Thanksgiving—Peter had been talking about going to the movies— but since Hal was skiing in Colorado with Kevin and Connor, I decided to stick around.

After the meal I even volunteered to wash the dishes. When the kitchen was clean, I headed upstairs to call Peter.

In our room Rose had just hung up the phone, and she looked like she was about to cry. "Stephen?" I guessed.

"There's got to be another girl," Rose said. "Why else would he be in such a hurry to get back to Harvard? 'Independent study project'—yeah, right!"

"Stephen wouldn't cheat on you."

Rose was chewing on a fingernail. "I hope not. I mean, he'd tell me if he wanted to go out with someone else, wouldn't he? Of course he would. We've always been completely honest with each other." She brightened. "I could just ask him, right? If I tell him what's on my mind, maybe he'll tell me what's on his."

"In the meantime can I use the phone?" I asked.

"First look at this." Rose opened a big photo album that was lying on her bed. "I dug this out of the closet downstairs—I'm going to show Mom. Look at this picture of your very first Christmas, Daisy!"

In the photograph I was sitting on Mom's lap—she looked so young—wearing a red-and-white-striped stretchy suit. I was as bald as an egg. "Look at my chubby cheeks," I said, laughing.

Rose flipped ahead in the album. "Look at us here. Matching velvet dresses."

"I hated those dresses. And the lace tights. Ugh!"

"This is more like it." Rose pointed to another picture of me. I was about eight, standing in front of the Christmas tree with a basketball tucked under one arm and a soccer ball under the other one.

She closed the album. The trip down memory lane seemed to be over, so I reached for the telephone. Before I could dial Peter's number, though, Rose said quietly, "You've changed so much, Daisy. Since you started dating Peter. You used to be so . . ."

"Wholesome?" I supplied sarcastically.

"That's not necessarily a bad thing, you know."

"Maybe I've just discovered that there's more to life than soccer," I told her.

"That's fine, but when you're with Peter, you—"

"Get off his case," I said. "It's not like you're such a relationship guru, anyway, Rose. You just said it yourself—things aren't so hot between you and Stephen these days."

"Yeah, okay, my relationship with Stephen isn't perfect," she admitted. "But my standards are really high. Being with Stephen has made me a better person because he respects me and expects a lot from me."

"Spare me the sermon," I said, but on some level Rose's words hit home. I couldn't pretend that Peter brought out the best in me. I thought about the stolen case of beer. Had loving me changed *him* for the better?

"Okay, sorry," Rose said. "I shouldn't preach. I

mean, I've dated some not so great guys. Remember Parker Kemp?" She laughed, then got serious again. "I thought I was in love with him, but he made me feel about two feet tall."

"My self-esteem is fine," I said.

"Is it?"

I shrugged. "Well, what if it isn't?"

Rose was looking at the photo album again. "Our first Christmas after Dad died," she said softly.

I didn't want to look at the picture. "Put that away," I told her.

"That was a hard time for me," Rose recalled. "All the adjustments. But you were always so . . . together. Happy Daisy. Responsible, unselfish, perfect."

"I was never perfect," I told her.

"Yeah, well, you *acted* like you were."

"Because you guys expected me to be that way."

Rose tilted her head thoughtfully. "Maybe. But we only *expected* it because you already *were*. Perfect," she added. "But you're showing us, huh?"

"I'm not trying to prove anything," I said.

"Good." Rose shut the photo album. "Okay, I'll get out of your hair. Make your phone call."

As Rose left the room I could hear Christmas music downstairs. Then the door closed, and it was quiet.

I started to call Peter but put the phone back down before I'd finished dialing. Rose was right about something. In the past few months, since I'd turned sixteen, I *had* made a 180-degree turn. Now I stared out the window at the winter dusk. I've stopped being perfect, I thought, but has that made me happy?

Eleven

The second half of my junior year started after New Year's. It was weird not having much to do. For the first time since I'd entered high school, I hadn't made honor society, and I wasn't playing basketball. People had stopped asking me to join clubs and be on committees.

Coach Wheeler hadn't given up on me, though. One Wednesday he called me to his office again, but I never got around to stopping by. I was on my way out the door after school when he came running after me. "Got a minute, Daisy?" he asked.

I shrugged. "Sure."

"What do you think about going to Patsy's with me? I skipped lunch today."

I shrugged again. "Yeah, okay."

We drove into town in Coach Wheeler's red Honda Civic. At the diner we picked a booth by a sunny window and both ordered clam chowder. "How's the knee?" Coach Wheeler asked me as he dumped a packet of oyster crackers in his soup.

"Still a little stiff," I answered.

"So, I was thinking about spring," he said. "If you start a conditioning regimen now, you'll be in

shape for softball, and it's going to be a fun season—
we're planning a trip to Florida during spring vacation. I have a friend who's a physical therapist—a
trainer at the state university gym—and he'd work
with you for free. Then maybe a couple of slow,
easy jogs a week or the Exercycle in the school
weight room. How does that sound?"

I took a sip of my soda, not sure how to answer.
I'd pulled so far away from that world. Did I want to
go back? "It sounds like a lot of work," I said at last.

"Absolutely," he conceded. "You're starting over,
basically. But you'll probably be voted cocaptain
this year. The team needs you. And I think you
need the team."

"Believe it or not, I've been doing okay without
sports," I said dryly.

Coach Wheeler looked at me. "Have you?"

Dropping my eyes, I fidgeted with my spoon.
Then I opened a packet of crackers and started
crumbling them. "I'll think about it," I said after a
minute, still not meeting his gaze. "About the conditioning thing."

He nodded. "Good enough. You know, I don't
mean to hound you, Walker, but I miss you. You never
come to see me anymore. How's stuff at home?"

"Okay," I said.

"Your mom's business is good?"

"Yeah, she's really busy. It's cool—she has to turn
down jobs sometimes now, she has so much stuff on
the calendar. But the thing that really bugs me—" I
stopped abruptly.

"What?" he prompted.

I hadn't intended to blab about my personal life, but since I'd started, I decided to finish. "It's Mom's boyfriend. Hal. They're really getting serious, and he's *always* at our house, and it drives me crazy because it's like he thinks he's already our stepfather or something. You know, helping us with our homework, telling us what to do."

"You used to let *me* boss you around and give you advice," Coach Wheeler said.

"Yeah, but you're not dating my mom," I pointed out.

He didn't reply, but he gave me this look he has—in fact, on the soccer team we always called it The Look, as in, "I'm getting The Look." It's this coach thing, and it kind of means, "What do *you* think you should do?" as in, figure it out yourself.

So I thought about it, and it started to seem pretty obvious. I'd liked Hal before he started dating my mom. And now I hated his guts because I didn't want him to marry my mother and become my stepfather. I didn't want *anyone* to be my stepfather.

And I was mad at my mom for the same reason.

Coach Wheeler had polished off his chowder. "How's that boyfriend of yours?" he asked as he took a couple of bucks out of his wallet to pay the check.

It had been kind of a relief to talk about what was going on with me, and I thought about telling Coach the truth about Peter, too—that things weren't so hot in some ways. What would I say, though? I wondered. I don't even know where to begin.

"My boyfriend's great," I answered.

At the hospital on Saturday, I looked for Ben first thing. When I found out he was with his doctor and couldn't see me, I was surprised at how disappointed I felt. I'd been counting on him to cheer me up. Isn't it crazy that the most optimistic person in my life right now is a fifteen-year-old kid with a brain tumor? I thought.

I answered the phones for an hour and in between calls sorted mail for the doctors. Then Jody trotted over. "I need a favor from you," she said. "Melody, our candy striper, called in sick. I'm going to have the nurses take turns picking up the phone, and I want you to take over for Melody."

She pulled me to my feet before I could answer. Not that there was a question involved—she was giving orders. "What does Melody do?"

Jody smiled. "She assists me. She delivers meals, changes sheets, reads books, you name it. Ready?"

"Sure," I said.

As we passed the supply closet Jody tossed me a pink smock. I made a face. "Pink?" I said distastefully.

She laughed. "What were you hoping for, a Red Sox jersey?"

She gave me a list of tasks and basically threw me into the deep end. I put clean sheets on the beds in rooms 303 and 310. I brought a pitcher of fresh water to the boy in room 317 and read two chapters of *The Hobbit* to the girl in room 301. I played cards with a couple of kids in the patients' lounge and then had to run down the hall to help one of the nurses calm a crying child. "I hate getting my temperature taken, too," I commiserated with the little boy. "And that medicine really does look yucky. Let's pretend it's a chocolate milk shake. No, make that a superdouble chocolate fudge M&M's whipped cream vanilla strawberry baseball football basketball milk shake."

The kid took his medicine and actually smiled. Becky, the nurse, shook her head. "Want to deliver the rest of the meds for me?" she joked.

I rejoined Jody at the nurses' station. "There you are," she said. "Dr. Dimarco's in room three-eleven. Would you take these charts to her?"

Jody handed me a clipboard. I carried it down the hall to room 311. Dr. Dimarco was inside, examining a girl who looked about Lily's age.

"Is it tender here?" she asked, gently palpating the girl's abdomen. "Or here?"

"Ouch," the girl said.

I handed the clipboard to Dr. Dimarco, watching her make some notes. Despite the white lab coat and stethoscope, she looked too young to be a doctor—she had a long blond ponytail and freckles and she was wearing high-tops.

"We're going to run some more tests," Dr. Dimarco told the girl in the bed. "It might be your appendix. Let's bring your folks in here and talk to them, too." She turned to me. "You're Daisy?" I nodded. "Would you run to the family lounge and bring Mr. and Mrs. Seaver in here?"

I escorted the Seavers to their daughter's room, and then Jody nabbed me. "Lunchtime." She pointed to a cart. "All the trays have cards on them saying where they go. Can you manage?"

"No problem," I assured her.

I delivered the meals to the entire ward, taking a minute to chat with each kid. I'm good at this, I realized as I plumped pillows and poured juice. "Your head really hurts, huh?" I said to a ten-year-old boy. "I'll tell the nurse, and we'll get you something to take care of that." There was a note in my voice that I hadn't heard for a while: energetic, efficient, enthusiastic. I'd forgotten how much I liked feeling busy and useful.

Pushing the empty cart toward the elevator, I bumped into Dr. Dimarco. "Are you premed, Daisy?" she asked.

"I'm still in high school," I told her, kind of flattered that she'd mistaken me for a college student.

"Thinking about going into medicine?"

Having seen Dr. Dimarco with her freckles and sneakers, it was easier than I would have thought to picture myself in a white coat with a stethoscope. And what better work could there be than making sick people well again? "Yes," I said. "I am."

"How do I look?" Rose asked me the following Friday. "I borrowed the dress from Rox. How about perfume—should I borrow Laurel's Windswept?"

We were in our bedroom, and Rose was turning around in front of the mirror, tugging on the hem of the black dress and fluffing her hair like some crazed beauty pageant contestant. "Let me guess," I said. "Stephen's coming home."

"I haven't seen him since Christmas." Rose put on some lipstick and smiled at her reflection so she could see if she'd gotten any on her teeth. "This dress had better light some sparks."

The dress was short and close fitting with a scooped-out neckline. Rose has a great figure, and with her long blond hair cascading over her shoulders she looked like a cover girl. "If it were any hotter, you'd catch on fire," I said.

Rose smiled again, this time for real. "Good, because I—"

Just then the phone rang. Rose grabbed it. "Hello?" she asked. "Oh, Stephen. It's you!"

I flopped down on my bed, thinking I'd take a little nap before I went out with Peter. I assumed Rose would just confirm her plans with Stephen and hang up. Instead she sat down on the edge of her bed. "You're not coming?" I heard her say.

For a couple of minutes it was quiet. Then Rose said, her voice trembling a little, "There's someone else, isn't there?"

I sat up. Rose had her back to me, and as she listened to Stephen she hunched her shoulders forward in a self-protective way. She was whispering, but I could still hear. "I know the long-distance thing is hard, Stephen, but . . . well, what am I supposed to feel? . . . I guess if you want to try it that way, it *might* end up making our relationship stronger. . . ."

I fiddled around at my desk. Finally Rose hung up the phone. I turned around. She looked at me, tears brimming in her eyes. "He broke up with me, Daze." She snapped her fingers. "After two whole years, just like that!"

"What happened?"

"He started off by canceling the weekend. He's still in Cambridge, and something came up at the last minute, yada yada yada. So then I just came right out and asked him if there was another girl. And he said . . . he said . . ." She sniffled loudly. "There *is* someone. Hayley. Can you believe it? Hayley! I even met her while I was visiting! I should have known. . . ."

Rose started to cry in earnest. I'd never seen her so upset . . . not since Dad died, at least.

"He swore nothing had happened between them yet," Rose went on. "He says he wouldn't cheat on me. But he wants to ask her out. He wants us to 'see other people.' Of course, that's just another way of saying it's over."

Rose covered her face with her hands, her shoulders shaking. I felt helpless. What should I do? I wondered. It really was a shock. Rose and Stephen had been together for ages—I always figured they'd get married someday.

Sitting down next to her on the bed, I patted her back. "Maybe he just needs some space," I said.

"Maybe. I tried to be mature, you know? I said, 'Okay, let's try it this way for a while.' But what if . . ."

Her voice dropped to an anguished whisper. "What if I never see him again? He's my best friend, Daze. What will I do without him?"

I didn't know the answer, so I just hugged her. It was strange. My heart ached for my sister, but the ache also felt good. Rose needed me.

"It'll be okay," I told her, my chin on her hair. "It'll be okay."

I ended up staying home on Friday night to keep Rose company so she wouldn't be too depressed. We made brownie sundaes with tons of whipped cream and watched videos until past midnight. Peter and I got together the next day instead. He picked me up around lunchtime. "Is the mall okay?" he asked as I buckled myself into the passenger seat.

"It's such a nice day," I replied, "and my knee's feeling a lot better. How about going for a walk or something? You know, just to be outside?"

"Too cold," Peter said. "Let's just go to the arcade."

"If that's what you want." Peter popped in a tape. As we drove along I twisted in my seat to take a good look at him. I knew his face so well now, and I still found him incredibly handsome. But is he my best friend? I thought, remembering what Rose had said the night before about Stephen. Do Peter and I have a foundation like that?

We bought tokens at the arcade, or rather I did—Peter doesn't have a lot of money, and I usually have some from my job, so I don't mind spotting him sometimes. We started to play this game called

Annihilation. Video games are pretty antisocial—
Peter doesn't like to be distracted, so we don't usually talk—but today I decided to break the rules.
Best friends are supposed to share their feelings. "I
saw my coach the other day," I told him. "You know,
Larry Wheeler? He coaches softball, too. Anyway,
he's after me to get back in shape, and I think I
might do it. I mean, see this trainer he knows."

Peter shrugged one shoulder, his eyes glued to
the screen. "Huh," he grunted.

I decided to take that as a display of interest.
"Yeah," I went on. "Maybe it's something about
spring. I feel like I want to try stuff. Like this job at
the hospital. I might branch out from just answering
phones. Being around all those doctors—maybe I'll
be premed in college, you know? If I take AP biology
next year, I could place out of freshman science."

Peter shot me a surprised glance. "You're not
gonna get nerdy on me, are you?" he kidded.

"I used to be a good student," I reminded him.

"Until you found better things to do with your
time," he said. "Think you'd even get into AP bio?"

That was a good question. I wasn't having the
best year academically. "I don't know, but it won't
hurt to try."

"Whatever," said Peter, turning his focus back
on Annihilation.

I'd already lost my game, but he kept racking up
the points. For a while I watched him play. His hands
were so quick, and his eyes blazed with energy. What
would happen if he ever put his energy into some-

thing productive? I wondered.

"So, we got this flyer in the mail the other day," I said conversationally. "From the continuing education program at the community college where Rose goes. They have all these cool-sounding courses for people who want to get their high school equivalency—computer, literature. . . ."

I paused. Peter shot up a few more bad guys before saying, "And?"

"And I thought about you. That's all," I said. "You have so much potential, like the way you're so good at chess. You could study math and—"

"You sound like my aunt." Peter flicked his wrist, then cursed and slammed a hand on the machine. "Lost the game."

"Sorry," I said, flinching a little.

"Hey." Peter turned to me and lifted a hand to touch my face. "I shouldn't have yelled. I didn't mean to hurt your feelings. It's just . . . me and school. I've told you how it is. It's not a good combination."

"These classes might be different, though," I said. "More informal. You could study whatever you wanted."

"Maybe I'll give it a try." He put his arms around me. "If it'll make you happy."

I nodded, even though I wasn't sure it *would* make me happy. He'd gone along with me but not necessarily for the right reason. "Should we play another game, or do you want to get something to eat?" Peter asked.

"I'm hungry," I answered.

We headed out to the food court. "Amy's having a party tonight," Peter said. "I'll pick you up at eight, all right?"

Suddenly I had a really odd feeling. It was like the walls of the mall were closing in on me. I didn't want to go to Amy's party. Everybody would be drinking and smoking and having the usual unofficial competition to see who could be the crudest and most sarcastic, and that didn't seem particularly entertaining anymore.

"Actually, I'm helping my mom at a party she's catering," I fibbed. "Passing appetizers and stuff."

"Too bad," Peter said.

Waiting for our order at the pizza place, I wondered why I'd made up that story. I don't feel like going out tonight, I decided. It doesn't mean I don't love Peter.

As we picked a table and sat down to eat, though, I knew I couldn't just brush aside those feelings. Peter was part of that scene. It was where he wanted to be, and for months now I'd been willing to follow him there. Now it was as if I'd come to the end of a road and found out it was a dead end. I was ready to turn around and head back. What I didn't know yet, though, was whether Peter would follow *me*.

Twelve

I almost called Peter back that evening and told him I could go out after all, but I didn't. I didn't want to go out. I needed to talk—really talk to someone—but who?

Jamila? I considered, sitting at my desk with the phone in my hand. Kristin? I was so out of touch with them these days. They'd probably be shocked if I called up just to chat.

Instead I dialed a familiar number—the pediatric ward at the hospital. "Is this Maxine?" I asked. Maxine and I sometimes see each other when we're changing shifts at the reception desk. "It's Daisy."

"What's up?" she asked.

"Can you connect me to Ben Compton's room?"

"Ben is no longer with us," Maxine answered.

My heart stopped beating. No, I thought. Not Ben. He can't be dead. "Oh, my God," I whispered. "He was my friend."

"Oh, honey, I'm sorry. I should have phrased that differently—I didn't mean to give you a scare. He's gone home for a while. Do you have that number?"

I was so relieved, I almost slid off my chair. "Yes, I have it. Thanks, Maxine."

I hung up the phone, but I was still shaking a little. I didn't actually have Ben's home number. I could look it up, I thought, or call information. I didn't do either thing, though. I just sat there, feeling incredibly thankful. I hadn't realized Ben had come to mean so much to me, but for a few seconds there I'd stared into a frightening void. Everything had looked black. Now the world had color again, rich colors I hadn't noticed before: the pale coral paint of my bedroom walls, the aqua and lavender of the twilit sky out my window, the warm pink-gold hues of my own skin. I exhaled the breath I hadn't realized I'd been holding. Thank you, God, I thought.

"I need doughnuts," Rose declared the next morning.

Mom had just left for church with Laurel and Lily; Rose and I had stayed home. "Like, now?" I asked. Wissinger's Bakery was right downstairs, but we were still in our pajamas.

"Chocolate glazed," she said.

I knew she was still bummed about what had happened with Stephen, so I decided to be a good sister. "Give me two minutes to throw on some clothes."

"You're an angel, Daze."

It's amazing we all haven't gained a hundred pounds since we moved into this apartment— Wissinger's always smells so good, and it's tempting when you're on your way home to just grab a giant M&M's cookie or a piece of carrot cake. Today I had to wait in line for a few minutes—Mr. Schenkel, our old neighbor, was buying doughnuts, and so were a few other people. When it was my turn, I said hi to the girl behind the counter. "How's it going, Gabby?"

Gabrielle's a classmate of mine at South Regional. "Busy," she replied. "Doughnuts?"

"A half dozen. Three chocolate glazed and three jelly."

Gabby stuck the doughnuts in a white bag. "It must have been a wild night, huh?"

I pulled a couple of dollars out of my coat pocket. "What?"

"Aren't you still going out with that Paco guy?"

"Yes," I told her, "but I didn't see him last night."

Gabby's eyes brightened. Her name fits—she's a gossip.

"So you don't know."

"I guess not," I said.

Gabby leaned on her elbows on top of the glass display case. "He and Marcus were picked up by the cops."

"You're kidding!" I was shocked. I hated hearing about this from someone like Gabby, but I had to find out what had happened. "What for?"

"Someone robbed the convenience store on the Old Boston Post Road. A couple of guys in ski masks."

My eyes widened. "And they picked up Peter and Marcus?"

"Just for questioning," said Gabby. "I guess they let them go. There wasn't enough evidence to arrest them or anything like that. I heard about it from

Amy—she was here ten minutes ago, but she didn't know all the details."

"Wow," I said, a little bit dazed. "Peter would never do anything like that, but . . . I suppose he'll tell me what happened. Um, thanks. For the doughnuts."

"Sure. See you around," Gabby said.

Back upstairs Rose and I polished off five of the six doughnuts and two cups of coffee apiece, which I'd gotten totally addicted to in the past couple of months. I didn't tell Rose about my conversation with Gabby, obviously, because for all I knew, it was just a rumor, and the last thing I needed was for my family to have a worse opinion of Peter than they already had.

The story got out, though, and fast. Rose and I were still hanging out in the kitchen when Mom, Lily, and Laurel got home. "How was church?" Rose asked.

Mom didn't answer Rose's question. Instead she looked at me with a troubled expression. "I heard something disturbing at coffee hour after the service," she began.

"What?" asked Rose.

Right away I knew what Mom was going to say. "There was a robbery at Reiser's Store," she said, "and apparently Daisy's boyfriend was questioned about it."

"Questioned," I emphasized. "That's all."

"I'm upset about this," Mom continued.

"Why?" I asked, my tone confrontational. "Peter didn't have anything to do with it. They released him, didn't they?"

Mom was chewing her lip in this way she has when she's thinking really hard about something. "You're old enough to choose your own companions, Daisy. I can't forbid you to go out with Peter, but—"

"Don't even try, Mom," I cut in. I shoved away the plate with the last doughnut on it and jumped to my feet. "You have no right. And whatever happened to 'innocent until proven guilty'?"

"Daisy, I'd like to give Peter the benefit of the doubt, but according to Joe Devon's wife, Chrissy—Joe was the officer who questioned Peter and his friend—the boys were—"

"I can't believe it," I shouted. "This is what you talk about at church? How Christian of you!"

"Take it easy, Daisy," Rose advised.

"No, I won't take it easy," I said. "She's been out to get Peter from the beginning. I'm sick of your interfering and judging me, Mom. Stay out of my life, okay?"

"How dare you talk to me like that when I'm trying to help you?" Mom asked, her voice shaking.

"You call this *helping?*" I shook my head. "I wish I were eighteen instead of sixteen—I'd be out of here so fast."

Mom drew in a deep breath. "Go to your room, Daisy. Let's both take a break before we say more things we'll regret. We can talk later."

"There's nothing to talk about," I declared as I ran from the room. "Peter's innocent, and I'll prove it!"

*　　　*　　　*

Just go ahead and ask him, I counseled myself. He'll set the story straight, and then I can tell everyone to leave us alone.

It was Sunday afternoon, and Peter and I had met at the mall to see a movie. We bought some popcorn and slid into a couple of seats in the second-to-last row. "Uh, Peter," I said, grabbing a handful of popcorn, "I saw Gabby St. James at the bakery this morning, and she told me that last night you and Marcus—"

"Man, those dumb cops," Peter broke in. "We just happened to be driving by Reiser's, but they kept us at the station for an hour. Like they needed some Saturday night entertainment and we were it."

"You mean you didn't—"

"In a small town the police have nothing better to do than harass you," Peter said. "Supposedly it was just fifty bucks, anyway. Big deal, you know?"

I looked at him, but the lights in the movie theater were dimming—it was coming attractions time—so I couldn't read his expression. Did you do it, though? I wondered, remembering how coolly he'd walked out of the liquor store with the case of stolen beer. I struggled with my feelings. Ask him, part of me urged. Let it drop, another inner voice said.

Just then Peter leaned close to me, showing me something he'd pulled out of his pocket. "I picked up a course catalog at the continuing ed place," he whispered. "After the movie you gotta tell me what to take."

At that moment the movie screen lit up with

flashing, colorful images and sound boomed from the speakers. Peter took my hand, and I held on tight. I wanted so much to believe that he was a good person who'd gotten some bad breaks, that underneath his tough attitude he had a gentle heart. He'll take some classes, I thought hopefully. We'll study together. Our relationship will grow.

If I didn't ask about the robbery, I wouldn't find out. Maybe that was the way to go.

When I got home, Mom was in the kitchen. She called after me as I headed for the stairs, but I didn't stop.

She followed me up to my room. She was wearing an apron, and her arms were white with flour. She's baking, I thought. Pie crusts. "Daisy, I'm sorry we had a fight," she said.

I shrugged.

"Let's make a date to sit down and—"

"Peter didn't rob Reiser's," I told her, turning away, "and that's all I have to say. Excuse me, I want to be by myself."

After about ten seconds I heard my door shut. I glanced over my shoulder. Mom was gone.

I stared at the closed door. I had a feeling things between me and my mother would never be the same again.

Thirteen

===

A week passed, and then another. There was a short article in the local paper about the convenience store robbery, in which it said there were "no suspects." No suspects, I thought on Saturday afternoon as I stuck the newspaper in the recycling bin. That's as good a motto as any, I guess.

Mom was catering a brunch in Portland, and she wasn't back yet, but my sisters were home. Rose was playing the piano and talking on the cordless phone at the same time. Lily was watching TV in the next room. Laurel had emptied the living room bookshelves of about a thousand back issues of *National Geographic* and was cutting them up with scissors. "Did Mom say that was okay?" I asked Laurel.

"I checked with her," Laurel answered.

"What are you doing, anyway?" asked Rose, clicking off the phone and wandering over.

"Making a collage," Laurel explained.

"For Nathan?" Rose's tone was teasing.

Laurel grimaced. "Definitely not. We broke up."

"You did?" Rose said. "How come?"

Laurel was wearing grubby overalls, and her tangled hair looked as if it hadn't been brushed in days.

I didn't smell Windswept. "I just decided I don't care if everybody else is a couple—it's just not me."

"Good for you. There's nothing wrong with being single," Rose said with feeling.

"I thought you went out with that guy from your econ class last night," I said.

Rose shrugged. "Craig? Yeah, we had an okay time. But it's not going anywhere." For a second her face looked inexpressibly sad—I knew she was thinking about Stephen. "Which is okay because I think it's going to be cool not having a boyfriend for a while. Who needs the distraction, you know? This way I can study all the time and get my grade point up so I can transfer to a better college someday. I can work more hours at Cecilia's and save money for acting lessons. I won't have time for dates."

It sounded like a good argument, but she wasn't convincing—she turned away to wipe a tear from her eye. Before I could say anything, Lily bounced into the room. "Come watch this cool TV show about haunted houses with me." The rest of us stared at her. "What are you looking at?" she asked.

"You. What are you *wearing?*" Rose asked.

Lily looked down at her outfit, which consisted of a Japanese kimono, metallic gold high heels, and about fifty bangle bracelets. "Nothing much."

"What happened to the uniform?" Laurel wondered.

"What uniform?" asked Lily.

"The Lindsey, Talia, Kendall, and Kimberly uniform."

"I'm not hanging around with those guys

anymore, if that's what you mean," Lily informed us.

"Why not?" Rose asked.

"Because all they ever wanted to do was make lists of the boys they like and fill out surveys in *Seventeen* magazine about what's your favorite color of lipstick. They had no *imagination*," she concluded with an expressive roll of her eyes.

It's nice to see my sisters back to normal, I decided a few minutes later as I went up to my room. Well, Laurel and Lily, anyway. Rose was down about Stephen, but knowing her, she'd bounce back fast. She had a lot of self-confidence, and her life was full of friends and activities. That leaves me, I thought, walking over to the window and staring out at the gray winter sky. Wasn't I kind of wearing a uniform, too? The spiky dyed hair, the baggy black clothes. I'd done it to fit in with Peter and his crew. I'd never thought about the fact that they made such a point of not conforming that they were conformists in their own way.

I traded the window for the mirror over my dresser. I'm not the vain type, but now, looking at my reflection, I was almost overcome by a wave of nostalgia and regret. I missed my long blond hair and healthy glow. Even my eyes didn't look familiar anymore. The detached, cynical expression that I'd adopted since I'd started hanging out with Peter was like a mask.

I turned away from the mirror. This is me now, I told myself. Peter and I had a date that night, and for once I wasn't looking forward to it.

*   *   *

I was on my way out the door—Peter doesn't come in, we always meet down on the street—when Mom got home. She was lugging a bunch of stuff from the party she'd catered, so I took one of the platters and a bag of dirty table linens to help her out. It was kind of awkward because I've been avoiding her as much as possible lately, but I couldn't just stand there and watch her struggle.

We dumped everything on the kitchen table, and Mom let out a big sigh. "What would I do without Sarah Cavanaugh?" she asked, kind of talking to herself. "I think I'd better ask her to be my permanent assistant." Just then Mom noticed my jacket and gloves. "You're going out?"

"Yeah."

"With Peter?"

"Yeah."

"I wish—," she began.

"I'm sorry you don't like Peter, Mom. But it just so happens that I do."

"I don't not like Peter," Mom protested.

"But you wish I wasn't going out with him," I said.

"I think you'd be happier with a different boyfriend," Mom admitted. "But it's your decision. Hal said that when Kevin and Connor were your age, they—"

Anger bubbled up in me. "Who cares about Hal?" I burst out. "What does he have to do with anything? We were doing just fine without him. We don't need him."

For a minute Mom stared at me, her brows lifted and her eyes wide. Then she said quietly, "Maybe *you* don't need him, Daisy, but I do."

I stared back at her, not knowing how to respond. What could I say? You're a mother—you're not supposed to have needs. And if you fall in love with another man, what will that do to our memories of Dad?

Mom seemed to be waiting for something. "I'm going out," I managed to mutter as I walked fast to the door. "Don't wait up."

I hurried down the stairs as fast as my stiff knee would let me and out to the sidewalk. The February night was overcast, and I could see snowflakes beginning to fall in the circles of light cast by the streetlamps. Peter wasn't there yet, so I stood on the curb, bouncing up and down a little to keep warm while I waited for him.

When the car pulled up, I knew right away that something was weird. The headlights bobbled, as if Peter had hit a pothole or something. When he stopped, he hit the curb—I had to jump back. "Hey, watch it!" I yelled.

Peter leaned over to open the passenger side door. "Hi, Sleeping Beauty," he said, grinning up at me.

I started to climb in, then stopped. Glancing over the back of the seat, I saw a pile of empty beer bottles on the floor. "Have you been drinking?" I asked suspiciously.

Peter looked at me with innocent eyes. "Who, me?"

"Look, I'm not driving with you if—"

Peter grabbed my arm and pulled me into the car. "Come on, Daisy. Don't be a drag." He gave me a sloppy kiss that tasted disgustingly of alcohol. "Anyhow, I'm a better driver drunk than most people are sober."

"I still don't think—"

He stepped on the gas, and the car lurched away from the curb. I had no choice but to slam my door. "I'll be careful," he promised. "Have a beer. It'll put you in a better mood."

I buckled my seat belt. "No, thanks," I said stiffly.

Peter cranked some tunes as we headed out of town. "Is there a party?" I asked, thinking that I could bum a ride home with someone else, or if worse came to worst, call home and ask Rose to come get me.

"I thought it could just be us tonight," Peter answered, slipping his right arm around me. "Maybe we'll get past second base for once, huh?" He grinned. "Like that baseball metaphor, Miss Jock?"

All of a sudden the boy sitting next to me seemed like a stranger. I was almost scared to be alone with him. "Sure," I said, though I didn't mean it.

We were on the Old Boston Post Road. As we cruised by the convenience store that had been robbed a few weeks ago Peter laughed. "Ol' man Reiser bought himself a guard dog," he said. "Guess we scared him, huh?"

I turned in my seat to stare at him. "What?"

He shot me a wry glance. "It was just fifty

bucks, Daze. And for a good cause. I gave twenty of it to my aunt for the rent."

I gripped my hands together to keep them from shaking. "It *was* you and Marcus?"

"I never pretended to be a saint," Peter said.

"But Peter, robbing someone—"

"I mean, the man charges a fortune for a quart of milk," Peter rationalized. "He drives a brand-new Dodge Dakota. He's not hurting."

I stared at Peter, trying as hard as I could to see his point of view. Maybe it was just a prank, I thought. No one got hurt, and Mr. Reiser doesn't really need the money. But it didn't work. What Peter had done wasn't cool; it was wrong. I couldn't laugh it off. "Peter, I think we should go someplace where we can talk. Let's go to Patsy's—I'll buy you some coffee."

"Not if you're going to lecture me," Peter said. "I get enough of that at home."

But he flipped a U-turn, heading back to town. Before we got to Patsy's, though, he pulled abruptly into the parking lot of a dark building—the community center. "Why are you stopping here?" I asked.

"I started my continuing ed class," he told me. "Astronomy. I thought it would be cool, looking at the stars. But the instructor slammed us with a quiz right off the bat, and she had the nerve to fail me. Can you believe it?"

"Did you talk to her about it?" I asked. "Maybe she'll let you take it over if you—"

"Forget that." Peter slammed his fist on the

steering wheel and then swung open his door. "Continuing ed's a crock." Now he was out of the car, fumbling in the backseat for something. "Is that your window, Ms. Turner?" he shouted into the night. "Here, I've got something for you!"

Peter pulled back his arm and threw something. A second later I heard the sound of breaking glass. "Peter, stop!" I yelled. Ignoring me, he hurled another empty bottle at the community center's windows. More glass shattered, and an alarm went off in the building. I was crying now. "Peter, *please!*"

He just went for another beer bottle—he'd lost all control. I thought about grabbing his arm to keep him from throwing it, but I was afraid to touch him. He was acting so crazy. How did I know he wouldn't hurt me?

Another window shattered. Was he going to break every single one?

I didn't stick around to find out. Peter wasn't even looking at me—he didn't see me turn and run away from him and from the sound of breaking glass, away from the police siren in the distance. I ran as fast as I could. My lungs burned from the cold air, and my knee hurt because I hadn't used the muscles in so long, but it was a good hurt. For the first time in ages I was moving.

I ran all the way home.

Fourteen

When the sun came up in the east the next morning, turning the ocean silver, I was sitting at my window in my desk chair, watching it. I was still in my clothes—I hadn't been able to sleep.

I tried to be quiet as I walked back across the room to my bed, but I tripped over a shoe. Rose rolled over in her bed, her down comforter rustling. "Is that you, Daze?" she mumbled sleepily.

I dropped down on my mattress. "Yeah."

Rose sat up. "Why are you up so early?"

"Never went to bed," I admitted.

She blinked. "You're kidding."

"No."

"How come?"

I hadn't planned to tell anyone about Peter breaking the windows, especially not my family. Lily was the only one who'd ever really liked him, and she did only because of his pierced ear. Why make them think worse of him than they already did? But suddenly I was tired of being alone with what I was feeling. "Rose, it was awful," I began, my voice shaky. "He'd been drinking, and I didn't want to drive with him, but he . . ."

She listened to the whole story without interrupting. When I got to the part about the robbery at Reiser's Store, she bit her lip, but she still didn't say anything. When I was done spilling my guts, I just sat on the edge of my bed, my back hunched and my eyes on the floor. I felt completely drained and as empty as one of Peter's beer bottles.

I waited for Rose to say, "I told you so; he was never any good." Instead she got out of bed and came over and put her arms around me. "I'm sorry, Daze," she said softly. "I'm really sorry."

I didn't want to cry, but tears spilled from my eyes, anyway. "Why does it have to be like this?" I asked.

Rose sighed. "Loving someone can be *so* hard."

My head on my sister's shoulder, I nodded, more tears sliding down my face.

Later that morning the doorbell rang. I was doing sit-ups in the family room, watching TV. "Can you get that?" I shouted to whoever might happen to be in the apartment. A minute later the bell jingled again. Grumbling, I got to my feet and went to the door.

Peter was standing in the hall. His guitar was slung over one shoulder, and he was holding a bunch of flowers. Daisies. "Can I come in?" he asked, shifting his weight awkwardly from one foot to the other.

I nodded, pulling the door wider. "Sure."

No one seemed to be around, so I led him into the kitchen. We sat down at the table, facing each other. I looked at Peter, waiting for him to speak. His eyes were a little bit bloodshot, and there was stubble on his chin. "Daisy, I'm sorry," he said finally.

I didn't say anything. "I don't know what came over me last night," he went on. "I just kind of lost it, I guess. I didn't mean to scare you. I swear."

I still didn't say anything. Peter shoved the bouquet across the table toward me. "It was just a couple of windows," he said, smiling crookedly.

"Peter, it's more than that," I said, choking a little. "You know it is."

He dropped his head. "Yeah, well . . . So, I wrote you another song. Listen."

He pushed his chair back so he could cradle the guitar on his lap. Then he bent his head, his hair falling forward, and picked out a sweet, sad tune. "There are words, too," he told me, "but I'm still working on them. How about . . ." He began to sing, his voice low and raspy. "Sleeping Beauty in the night, breaks away, takes my light." He looked up at me, flashing the crooked smile again. "Crummy, huh?"

I'm really not the crying type—I'm not emotional and dramatic like Rose. But something about the song Peter had written for me, or maybe it was his smile or the way he held the guitar in a kind of embrace, made my eyes brim with tears. "Peter, I—"

"Say it's okay, okay?" he said. Then he laughed at himself. "Say it's okay, okay," he repeated. "Now, that could be in a song."

"Peter . . . it's not."

"It's not what?"

"Okay," I said. "It's not."

A shadow flickered across his thin, handsome face. "What are you saying? You don't mean it's over just because I got a little wild last night . . . do you?"

"I've been thinking about it for a while," I confessed. "About us. And I just think . . ."

I couldn't finish the sentence. In my heart I knew it was time for us to go our separate ways. I knew it was for the best. But I also knew it was going to hurt a hundred times more than tearing the ligaments in my knee.

"We could still be cool together," Peter said when I stayed quiet. "I love you, Daisy."

His voice was rough—I'd never heard him speak with so much emotion. I believed he was telling the truth. He did love me, in his own way. When I looked in his eyes, I felt the same attraction that had been there the very first day we met. *But it's still not right,* I thought.

"I'm sorry, Peter," I whispered.

"So, that's it?" he said in disbelief. "I should just leave?"

Not looking at him, I nodded.

I heard his chair scrape along the floor. His guitar bumped the table, the strings reverberating with a discordant sound. There were footsteps, and a door closing, and then nothing.

I slumped in my chair, my head dropping onto my folded arms, and began to cry. When I felt a hand on my hair a minute later, I jumped.

"Are you all right?" Rose asked.

I shook my head, sniffling. "No."

She knelt on the kitchen floor so she could give me a hug. "Believe it or not, the world will keep turning," she said. "You'll get over this."

I knew she was speaking from experience, but it didn't help. The first boy I'd ever really loved had just walked out of my life . . . because I'd told him to.

Mom had gone to the mall with Lily and Laurel, so for a while longer the apartment was quiet, which was a plus since I didn't feel like explaining why I was bawling my eyes out. By the time they got home, I'd stopped crying. Mom went right back out again with Hal, and Laurel headed over to Jack's—he'd broken up with Tammy, and they were friends again. I hid out in front of the TV. I never used to watch much before I met Peter—I used to be too busy—but he was a dedicated channel surfer, and now I clicked the remote, sniffling when I came across a commercial he and I had laughed over together or a music video he'd liked.

When the doorbell rang, I went to get it, bumping into Lily at the door. "Rose said you and Peter broke up," Lily whispered. "Do you think that's him, coming back to make up with you?"

I was wondering the same thing. "Oh, Lily, I hope not." But when I opened the door, it wasn't Peter. "Stephen!" Lily and I exclaimed together.

Rose had come downstairs just in time to hear us. She appeared in the front hall, her face pale and her eyes wide. "Stephen!" she said, sounding even more surprised than we were.

"Sorry to just drop in on you this way," he said, "but I was really hoping . . ." He glanced at me and Lily. "Um, do you think we could talk someplace private?"

"Sure," said Rose. "Let's go in the family room."

They walked off, and I heard Rose turn off the TV. Lily and I loitered in the hall, drifting casually toward the family room. Rose had closed the door but not all the way.

"I was going to call you, but then I thought, this is too important," Stephen was saying. "I had to see you. I want us to be together again, Rose."

"What about Hayley?" Rose asked, her tone cool.

"We went on a couple of dates," Stephen admitted, "and I like her, but it just didn't click. Whenever I was out with her, I'd spend the whole time thinking about you. It just made me realize how much I love you."

"Really?" Rose said, not sounding quite as frosty as before.

"Really." There was a brief pause, and I guessed he was putting his arms around her. "I hope I didn't hurt you, Rose. I mean, I think I needed some time to test this out. Thanks for giving me the space."

"I needed to experiment, too," she said. "I went out with this guy from school. But it was the same thing—you were on my mind all the time."

"God, I've missed you so much."

"Me too."

There was another pause—a long one. They're kissing, I thought happily. I looked at Lily. She mimed clapping and mouthed, "Yay!"

Just then Rose peeked around the door and saw us standing there. She didn't get mad, though—she was too blissed out. Smiling, she shut the door in our faces.

"And they lived happily ever after," Lily declared with satisfaction.

I nodded. It sure looked that way.

Stephen stayed for dinner, and it was like a holiday. Mom whipped up an incredible meal. Everyone was so glad to have him back in the family, it was almost sickening. He and Rose were completely moony—they were sitting next to each other at the table, and Stephen's a lefty, so they kept bumping elbows and giggling.

After dinner the lovebirds went for a drive. Lily and Laurel did their homework at the kitchen table while Mom and Hal watched *Masterpiece Theater* in the family room. I went up to my room, thinking I'd read my English assignment, but I couldn't concentrate. I kept picturing Peter's face and hearing his voice in my mind, singing the song he'd written for me.

What a day, I thought with a sigh as I sat on my bed, my back propped against the pillows. Peter and I break up, and Rose and Stephen get back together. I was glad for my sister, but her joy made me wistful—it was such a contrast to my own misery. But it was my idea to end things with Peter, I reminded myself. We could never have had the kind of solid relationship Rose and Stephen had.

Shifting on the bed, I reached over for the two small wooden picture frames on my night table. One held a photo of my father and the other one a photo of Peter.

As I stared at their faces my vision blurred with tears and my heart ached with a sense of loss so intense, I thought it would tear me in half. I'd kept my grief about Dad's death buried deep inside me for three whole years; now there was no holding it back.

Clutching the picture of my father, I rocked back and forth on the bed, sobbing. "I got to say good-bye to Peter, but I didn't get to say good-bye to you, Dad," I whispered. "You went out on the boat, and we never saw you again. We didn't even have a body to bury—just a stone at the cemetery with your name on it. Oh, Dad."

I continued weeping silently. Gradually my body stopped shaking. Sniffling, I wiped my wet eyes on the sleeve of my shirt. I drew in a deep, uneven breath, then let out a sigh that seemed to hold a lifetime's worth of emotions.

A weird feeling of peace settled over me. I put the pictures of Dad and Peter back on my night table. I knew I'd never completely get over the pain of losing my father—there would always be things I wanted to share with him, questions I needed to ask him. Memories were thin compared to the real thing, but memories were going to have to be enough.

Poor Mom, I thought suddenly. Trying to be a

mother *and* a father to the four of us. Dad didn't beat around the bush—if he'd still been around, he'd probably have come down a lot harder on me than she did.

My eyes grew misty again, but I smiled. "You'd have set me straight, wouldn't you, Dad?" I said aloud.

Instead I was going to have to do it on my own.

Fifteen

"One more lap," Kristin panted as we rounded the far turn on the high school track.

"Think you can make it?" Jamila asked me.

"Yeah," I huffed. "No sweat."

It was an afternoon in early April, and we were working out to get in shape for the spring sports season. Jamila runs track and Kristin plays tennis, and they'd both slacked off over the winter—I wasn't the only one making up for lost time.

We'd started out just jogging, but now, as we headed into our final lap, we all pushed a little harder. Kristin sped up, so Jamila and I did, too. Then I gave it a little more gas, and they kept pace with me. We're all supercompetitive—no way did any of us plan to lag behind.

As we entered the home stretch we were sprinting full out, staying exactly abreast of one another. At the finish line, though, I'm pretty sure I was ahead by an inch or two.

We collapsed on the infield grass, laughing and groaning. "You guys are killing me," I said breathlessly.

"That's what Coach Wheeler told us to do," Jamila huffed.

She and I flopped on our backs. We were wearing sweats, but the grass was cold and damp. "Come on, get up," Kristin ordered, "or your muscles'll tighten up."

She gave me a hand and hauled me back onto my feet. We walked a brisk lap of the track, then did some stretching. "I almost forgot I *had* muscles," I said as I leaned against a bench to stretch my calves and Achilles tendons.

Kristin was bending sideways to stretch her waist, her long red braid hanging almost to the grass. "Do you hear from Peter?" she asked.

It had been over a month since we'd broken up. "No," I admitted.

"That must hurt," Jamila said.

I nodded. It hurt a lot.

My friends were quiet for a few minutes. I was glad they didn't ask any more questions about Peter or about everything else that had gone on with me the past few months. Maybe at some point I'd feel like talking about it, but not right now, and they seemed to sense that.

We finished our cooldown and walked back to the gym. I took deep breaths of the fresh air. The trees were still bare, but the days were getting longer and a little warmer. Last fall when I'd hurt my knee, I'd thought spring would never come, but here it was.

"Just like the good old days," Kristin said.

"I was just thinking that," Jamila agreed.

I smiled at them. "Thanks for letting me back in the club."

"Are you kidding?" said Kristin. "It wasn't right with only the two of us."

"We were lazy without you," Jamila confirmed. "Extra butter on our popcorn at the movies and zero exercise."

I slung one arm around Jamila's shoulders and the other around Kristin, leaning my weight on them. I remembered how they'd helped me off the field after I injured my knee. They were still holding me up. "Well, from now on," I said, "we're hard-core."

"Super-hard core," said Kristin.

"You better believe it," said Jamila.

"Although you guys still have to buy a bunch of the candy bars I'm selling to raise money for the softball trip to Florida," I reminded them.

"Put me down for five," Kristin said. "I swear I'll give them to my brothers."

We were almost to the gym. Suddenly I felt like running again. I took off at a dead sprint, with Jamila and Kristin tearing after me. "Last one to the showers is a smelly old jockstrap!" I shouted back to them.

A couple of nights later I was working at the hospital. Whenever nurses and doctors stopped by the reception desk, I hit them up to buy candy bars for the softball team fund-raiser. An hour into my shift a call came in for me. "Ben!" I said cheerfully.

"Just thought you might be bored," he said.

"You can't fool me," I teased. "You miss this place."

"No way," he said with feeling. "It's a zillion times better being an outpatient."

Another call came in and I put him on hold. "Don't you have anything better to do?" I asked when I punched his line again.

"Nope," he said.

"So, tell me what you think. Jody mentioned the job again, you know, organizing activities for the ward, and I think I might do it. Do you think kids would like puppet shows?"

Ben and I chatted about the possibilities. Then we talked about opening day in the major leagues and school—I was studying my brains out these days, trying to pull my grades back up. Ben thought he might want to do premed, too. "Maybe I'll do research," he said. "Find a cure for cancer."

"Why not?" I said.

"Well, I'll let you do your homework. I just wanted to make sure you weren't too bummed about Peter."

"Yeah, well . . ."

"I'm not going to get mushy on you," he swore. "Don't get the wrong idea here. But you are possibly the most beautiful, coolest, nicest, smartest girl I've ever met, Daisy. Okay? Bye now."

Ben hung up fast. Blushing a little and smiling also, I replaced the receiver. "What's so funny?" Jody asked as she stepped up to get her phone messages.

"Life," I replied.

*   *   *

Driving home later that night, I found myself detouring way out of the way toward the mall in Kent. I don't know why—maybe because the song on the radio reminded me of Peter. I hadn't planned this, but as I parked and walked inside to the video arcade I really hoped I'd find him there. I needed to see him one more time.

There was a guy playing Annihilation, but at first I didn't think it was Peter because he had a crew cut. Then I got closer and recognized my ex-boyfriend. "Hey," I said, suddenly feeling shy.

Peter glanced at me, then back at the game, and then did a double take. "Daisy! Hey."

He hit pause and turned to face me. He slouched against the machine; we didn't touch. "What are *you* doing here?"

"I was heading home from the hospital, and I had this craving for a strawberry-banana smoothie from Juice Junction," I fibbed. "I'm working out a lot for softball, and I get starving."

"You look good," he said.

"So do you." I smiled. "I almost didn't recognize you, though."

Peter put a hand to his chin. Along with the crew cut, he was working on a scraggly goatee. "Yeah, it's my new look for spring. And you're blond again."

"Yeah," I said. My hair was growing out, and I'd had the dyed part trimmed off. It was kind of nice not to jump every time I looked in the mirror anymore. "It matches my eyebrows—that's a plus. So, what are you up to these days?"

"Mom's on this new medication and she feels really good, so she's been on me to look for a job. I just found something—riding around on a recycling truck. I start tomorrow."

"Cool," I said in an encouraging tone.

He shrugged. "Yeah, well, we'll see. It's a paycheck. I've been thinking about getting out of here, though, you know? Maybe move to Portland or Boston. Someplace where there's a little more action."

"Yeah?"

"Yeah." Another shrug. "But whatever."

I nodded. "Well."

"Well," Peter echoed.

For a minute we just looked at each other. We'd run out of things to talk about. "I guess I'll go grab that smoothie," I said at last.

"Okay," he replied. "Take it easy."

"You too."

I lingered a few seconds longer. Shouldn't we be crying or fighting or hugging or something? I wondered. But I couldn't think of anything else to say. The emotion just didn't seem to be there for either of us.

That's what made the tears jump into my eyes. Not that Peter and I had broken up but that I didn't miss him nearly so much as I'd thought I would. That my first love could die so quickly.

I turned away before he could see that I was crying and jump to the wrong conclusion. "See ya," I said as casually as I could manage.

He'd already turned back to his video game. "Yep."

As I left the arcade, though, with my shoulders square and my chin up, I had a feeling I wouldn't ever see Peter again.

The first South Regional High girls' softball game was held on a damp April Wednesday after school. Thanks to the misty, cold weather the home bleachers were nearly empty, which is why I couldn't help noticing the woman with the yellow umbrella.

Mom.

She cheered right until the last inning, when I batted a triple to bring in the winning run. My teammates and I hopped all over one another, congratulating ourselves on our first victory of the season, and then lined up to shake hands with the Eastport team, who weren't quite so happy about how things had turned out. Then while we all pulled on sweatshirts and slickers, Mom came up with a big Tupperware container full of oatmeal-raisin cookies.

The team descended on the cookies as if they hadn't eaten in a week. Coach Wheeler grabbed one, too. "Thanks, Mrs. Walker," everybody said.

I didn't take a cookie, and I didn't say anything. I felt pretty awkward, in fact. Mom had shown up at the game as if there weren't any tension between us—as if we were some totally tight mother-daughter act, when in fact we'd hardly talked in months.

The rest of the team was starting to drift toward the gym and a hot shower. I got ready to bolt, too, but before I could take a step, Coach Wheeler grabbed my arm. "What?" I asked. He didn't explain himself.

He just kept shoving me . . . in Mom's direction.

Coach Wheeler and the softball team disappeared. Mom and I were suddenly alone on the deserted field. The drizzle had stopped, so she folded up her umbrella. "Great game," she said.

"Yeah."

There had been a question in Mom's voice. I'm not sure what she was asking, but I guess she got the right answer. One of us took a step, anyway, and then we were hugging. "I've missed you, Daisy," she whispered.

"I know. I'm sorry," I whispered back.

We hugged a little more, both of us sniffling, and then we started laughing. Mom's umbrella was between us and it was practically stabbing me. "Let's sit in the bleachers," she suggested. "It's not too wet."

We found a dry spot—the sun was actually peeking out from behind a cloud. Mom put the Tupperware on the bench between us, and we each munched a cookie. "I haven't had a chance to tell you that I'm sorry things didn't work out with Peter," Mom said.

"It's probably for the best," I told her. "We didn't have that much in common. And anyhow, you can't *really* be sorry."

"It was a tough position to be in for me as a parent," she said. "I wish I'd handled things differently. I shouldn't have alienated you like that."

"I did a pretty good job of alienating myself," I assured her.

"Well, sometimes I thought you were only dating Peter to punish me," Mom confessed. "How self-centered could I get!"

"Why would I want to punish you?" I asked.

Mom reached for another cookie and broke it in two. "Because of Hal."

"Well, you didn't like Peter, and I'm not crazy about Hal," I said. She offered me half of the cookie, and I took it. "That makes us even."

"Why don't you like Hal, though?" Mom asked. "He's trying so hard with you girls."

"Maybe he's trying *too* hard."

Mom was silent for a moment. Then she said quietly, "Being in a relationship with another man doesn't mean I've forgotten your father. I loved Jim. I'll always love him, and he'll always live for me in my daughters. Especially you."

I had to fight through my tears to get the words out. "I hate it, though. That Dad's just a memory. Every day I want him back with us."

"I know," Mom said.

"I don't want him to live in me," I went on. "I want him to live."

"I know," Mom said again, and reached for my hand. Tears were streaming down my face. I took a deep breath. "Well," I said shakily, "I'm sorry I've been giving you a hard time about having a boyfriend. It just takes some getting used to."

"Sure. I understand."

We finished the last couple of oatmeal cookies. "I can't believe I ate that," Mom said with a laugh.

"That's my cardinal rule—don't eat what you cook. If I tasted everything, I'd be a blimp."

I smiled at her. "You're not a blimp, you're a babe," I told her. "No wonder Hal couldn't resist you."

Mom stood up. "I don't know about that, but I'll tell you, I *do* feel young sometimes. Like I've had a chance to start my life over."

"What do you mean?"

"Well, things couldn't have seemed worse to me after your dad died. But that chapter ended, and another one began. I've decided that's what life is like—a book," Mom said. "And every time we start a different chapter, we get to be a different person, too. I used to be a housewife and a mom, and now I have my own business. The other day I officially hired Sarah—I'm an employer! Who'd have thought it?"

"It's pretty amazing," I agreed. I thought about how *I'd* tried being a different person for a while.

"Anyway," Mom concluded as we walked to her parked car, "I guess the important thing is to be who *you* want to be and not who other people want you to be."

"You mean, like peer pressure?" I asked.

"Or like what your parents might expect," she said. "I know sometimes I asked too much of you, and I'm sorry for that."

"It's all right," I said. "I liked feeling needed."

"Of course I need you," Mom said. "That's not going to change. But let's find a happy medium, okay?"

We climbed into the car. Mom tossed her umbrella

and the Tupperware in the backseat—I fiddled with the radio. "Hey, what happened to my station?" Mom protested as rock music blasted from the speakers.

"That boring classical stuff?"

"Come on." She laughed. "There's got to be a—"

"Happy medium?" I finished. I grinned. "Okay, I'll settle for oldies."

We drove home, both of us humming to the Beach Boys, and I realized for the first time in ages that my knee didn't hurt. I'd finally healed.

Sixteen

The day before Easter my sisters and I gathered in the kitchen to color eggs, as we do every year. We each had half a dozen, and we took turns sticking them in cups of vinegar with purple, pink, green, blue, yellow, and orange dye.

"You've got to leave it in for longer or it's too pale," Laurel advised Lily as Lily scooped an egg out of the pink dye.

"I like it this way," Lily insisted, placing her egg carefully in the egg carton and then dropping another one in the blue cup. "It's understated."

"It's *white*," said Laurel.

"Just because you leave your eggs in for an *hour*," Lily said.

"Time out," I told them. "Can't we have a little harmony here?"

Rose got up from the table to open the window over the sink. "Doesn't it smell like spring?" she asked happily.

It *was* a beautiful April day. Crocuses were blooming in the park, and the ocean was a softer blue. "And I heard you and Jack have spring fever," she added, looking at Laurel as she sat back down at the table.

"What did you hear?" Laurel asked, blushing fiercely.

"Well, Rox's cousin Rachel was at that party with you guys last night, and Rachel told Rox that you and Jack spent a *long* time in the kissing closet. And Rox told me, naturally."

"We were playing spin the bottle," Laurel said defensively. "We *had* to go in the closet—that's the rule."

"And?" Rose pressed.

Laurel dumped an egg in the green cup, splashing dye all over the newspaper covering the table. "Well, we were just going to sit in there and count to fifty," she said, "but then we thought we should just kiss fast because that way we wouldn't have to lie about it, but then he, like, kissed me for *real.*"

Laurel looked disgusted. I tried to hide my smile as I remembered how *I* felt about the opposite sex back in eighth grade. "Was it awful?" I asked sympathetically.

"It was totally gross," Laurel confirmed.

"Jack's so cute, though," Rose said. "I'd think he'd be a great—"

"We're just friends, okay?" Laurel said.

"The kiss didn't chase you off?" I asked.

"I made him promise he'd never ask me out again," Laurel explained. "Well, at least not for a few years."

"In a few years you might change your mind about kissing," Rose predicted in a knowing tone.

"I doubt it," Laurel declared.

We finished coloring the eggs, leaving them to

dry in the egg cartons. "Who's up for a game of catch in the park?" I asked.

It turned out that everyone was. We grabbed a bunch of mitts and a softball and headed outside.

"What's happening with that spring break trip, anyway?" Rose called as she lobbed the ball to me.

"The team's going to a tournament in Florida," I answered, tossing the ball to Lily. "We've raised some money selling candy bars and doing car washes, but everybody has to pitch in three hundred bucks. I'd like to go, you know? Now that I'm back into the sports thing. Bonding with the team and all that. But I haven't saved up enough. I have, maybe, one-fifty." I was disappointed but not *really* disappointed. There would be other trips, and it wouldn't be a bad thing for me to spend spring vacation studying.

"Hmmm," said Rose. "That's too bad."

"Yeah, well, maybe next year," I said.

We played catch for fifteen minutes and then headed back inside, discussing what we were going to wear to church the next morning. "Stephen's coming to the service with us, so I think I'll wear my light blue dress since it's his favorite," Rose said.

"I'm going to wear my light yellow dress with the white collar," I said.

"It's so good to see you abandoning black," Rose exclaimed. "Don't you want to hear what I'm going to wear?" Lily asked.

"Of course," I said.

"I sewed the lace back on that old-fashioned

pink dress we found in Great-grandma's trunk," Lily began. "And I'm going to wear white gloves and a straw hat with a long pink ribbon."

"You'll look like Little Bo Peep," I predicted.

Lily ignored me. "And I have a little pink beaded purse to carry my offering in and a white velvet cape the lady at Second Time Around sold me for only three dollars, and I'm going to pin a sprig of lily of the valley to the breast of my gown as an emblem of spring."

"You'll be a vision," Rose said, winking at me.

I smiled. Lily's outfit sounded ridiculous, but I felt like hugging her. It was just so good to be back to normal—all four of us. I was kind of bummed that I wouldn't be able to go on the softball trip, but in the grand scheme of things, that was pretty minor.

Life was as it should be.

"Leg of lamb with rosemary and mint jelly," Rose gushed.

"And scalloped potatoes," Laurel said. "My absolute favorite."

"The asparagus is what I'm looking forward to," Hal said. "Your mother cooks it perfectly."

We were home from church, and Mom was making a special midday Easter dinner because later we were all going to the hospital to help with the Easter egg hunt I'd organized for the children's ward.

"Lily, would you set the table?" Mom asked. "Use the good china."

"How about flowers and candles?" Lily asked.

"The candles are in the pantry," Mom replied, "and the flowers . . ." She put a hand to her forehead. "I knew I forgot something when I was shopping yesterday. Flowers!"

"There are a ton of daffodils growing at the edge of the park," I said. "Do you think anyone would care if we picked a few?"

"Maybe just a handful," Mom said. "It *would* brighten up the table."

I started toward the door. Before I could leave, Hal joined me. "I'll walk to the park with Daisy," he announced. "Then I can grab that bottle of wine from my fridge on the way back."

He and Mom exchanged a significant glance. "You don't have to," I told Hal, not exactly psyched at the prospect of a chat with him.

"No, it's okay," he assured me. "While you're picking daffodils, I'll stand guard in case any local law enforcement passes by."

It looked like I was stuck with Hal, so instead of arguing, I jogged down the stairs and then hurried along the sidewalk with brisk strides. Hal practically had to run to keep up with me.

"Daisy, I'd like to talk to you," he said as we got to the park.

"No kidding," I replied with a trace of my old Peter-style sarcasm.

Hal grinned. He's geeky looking, with his glasses and receding hairline, but for the first time I noticed that he had a nice smile. I could *almost* imagine what Mom sees in him. "I'm not Mr. Subtle," he acknowledged. "It's just, you and I . . . we haven't had an easy time of it since your mother and I started dating."

"She's the one who's going out with you, not me," I pointed out as I bent over to pick some daffodils.

"Right." Hal stood off to the side, his hands stuck in the pockets of his gray flannel trousers. "But it's important to me to have a good relationship with you and your sisters."

Well, then you shouldn't always butt into our lives and tell us what to do, I thought. I didn't say anything out loud, though. I knew he wanted some encouragement, but I couldn't bring myself to say, "We're all wild about you, especially me."

Hal broke the silence. "The thing is, Daisy, I know how hard it's been for you to lose your dad. My father died from a heart attack when I was in college."

I straightened up, clutching a handful of daffodils. How did Hal know that had been bothering me? I wondered. But I still didn't say anything.

"I missed him for a long time," Hal went on. "Still do every now and then. Kevin and Connor never got to know him."

I nodded.

"I guess I just want you to know that whatever happens between me and your mom—if we really start getting serious, and I hope we do—I don't aim to take your dad's place. No one can do that."

I cleared my throat. "Well . . . thanks," I said lamely.

"And if I ever seemed kind of high-handed, I'm sorry," he concluded. "It's just that I had a houseful of boys, and I'm used to bossing people around."

"It's okay," I said, and suddenly, it was.

Hal glanced around. "I don't see any cops." Bending, he plucked a flower. "Happy spring, Daisy," he said, holding it out to me.

I took the daffodil and smiled at him. "Same to you."

Easter dinner was delicious, naturally. "I ate so much, I don't have room for dessert," Lily complained at the end of the meal.

"Not even cheesecake with fresh strawberries?" Mom asked.

"Well . . . maybe a *little* piece," Lily said.

"Aren't you glad you're not still a vegan?" Rose asked her.

Lily laughed. "Am I ever."

Mom served dessert and hot tea. When everyone had a slice of cheesecake, Rose clinked a spoon against her water glass. "Attention, please," she said. "I have an announcement."

"What is it?" asked Stephen, who was sitting to her left.

She bumped him with her elbow. "*You* know, but no one else does." She turned to Mom. "Okay, guess what I did a couple of months ago?"

Mom gave Rose a bemused smile. "I have no idea, but you've got me curious."

Rose leaned over to Stephen so she could hook her arm through his. "You know how hard I've been working in my classes. I got all A's last semester."

"I know, and I'm very proud of you," Mom said.

"Well, I applied for a scholarship." Rose paused dramatically. "At Boston University. And . . . they invited me for an audition in the music and drama department. And . . ." She paused again.

"What happened, Rose?" Lily squeaked excitedly. "Did you get it?"

Rose broke into a smile. "I got it. I got the scholarship! I'm transferring to BU in the fall!"

We all cheered loudly. "Yahoo!" I yelled.

"Rose, that's wonderful!" Mom exclaimed.

"Isn't it great?" Stephen was beaming. "Boston University. Right across the Charles River from Harvard!"

"What a coincidence," Hal said, grinning.

"So, that's not all," Rose said when we'd quieted down.

"What else?" Mom wondered.

"Well, you know how I've been saving money for acting lessons," Rose said. "I have enough now, and I'm taking lessons in Portland starting next week."

"Congratulations," Mom said. I was sitting on Rose's other side, and I high-fived her.

"That's not all, though," Rose told us. She looked at me. "I have some money left over. A hundred dollars. I want you to have it, Daze. For the Florida trip."

"You're kidding," I said.

"No. And Hal has something to add," she said.

"Fifty dollars," Hal said. "Rose told me that would be enough to make up the total, along with your own savings."

"What?" I looked from Rose to Hal and back again. They were smiling. "I can't believe you guys."

"You've always done so much for me and for the whole family," Rose said. "It's the least I can do."

I blinked back a tear. "Thanks," I told her. I turned to Hal. "Thank you so much."

"You're welcome," he said.

Mom lifted her wineglass. "I think this is a good time for a toast." Hal raised his wineglass, too, and my sisters and I lifted our water glasses. Mom looked at me and then at Rose. "Here's to softball trips and scholarships." Her gaze moved to Lily and Laurel. "And Easter bonnets and kissing closets."

"Hey, who told?" Laurel yelped indignantly.

"Here's to my family," Mom concluded, smiling. Her eyes were on Hal's now. "And to the future."

"Here, here," said Hal.

I clinked my glass with Rose's. "Cheers," I said.

After dinner we washed the dishes and then packed up the car with food Mom had made for the party at the hospital, along with bags of Easter candy and stuffed rabbits donated by people from church. When we got to the hospital, Laurel and I set up the Easter egg hunt while Mom put out the food and Rose and Lily did face painting for the little kids. It turned out to be a pretty fun party—the kids had a great time hunting for candy and eggs.

At one point Ben joined me. Rose had painted a rainbow across his cheeks and nose. "Nice face," I commented.

"Where's *your* paint?" he asked.

I laughed. "I've gotten the urge to dye myself strange colors out of my system."

Ben pulled up a chair so he could help me pour jelly beans into bowls. "Guess what?"

"What?"

"I'm better."

I tilted my head to one side. Ben had been sick the whole time I'd known him. "What do you mean?"

"Better," he repeated. "As in 'full remission.' As in I'm finishing up this round of outpatient treatment and then I'm done. For good."

"Ben, that's the best news I ever heard!" I threw my arms around him, tears sparkling in my eyes. "I'm so glad!"

"So, what do you say?" Ben wriggled away from me. He's not the touchy-feely type. "It'll take me a couple of months to get back in shape, but this summer I should be biking and stuff again. I'll race you up Mountain Road—how does that sound?"

I pictured Ben healthy again, with color in his face and meat on his bones and hair on his head. I thought about the year I turned sixteen and all the things I'd learned working at the hospital. I thought about how I'd said good-bye to Peter, my first real love, but at the same time I'd made a friend like Ben. I thought about my fights with Mom and how we were getting along better than ever. I thought about Dad and how I'd always, always miss him.

What a wonderful world it was. I couldn't wait

for the softball trip to Florida. And next year I'd
visit Rose at BU and apply to colleges myself.
Maybe I'd get an athletic scholarship. I'm going to
go for it, I thought. No more pretending to be someone I'm not.

"It sounds great," I told Ben as we helped ourselves to handfuls of jelly beans. Remembering
Mom's toast, I added, "Here's to the future."

My sisters and I: we'd be together forever. At least, that's what I thought, until the year I turned sixteen. That's when my older sister, Daisy, died.

Daisy had always been the glue that kept the family together. Without her, we were falling apart. Luckily, I had someone to talk to—Jack.

But after he helped me through the hardest time of my life, Jack confessed that he wanted to be more than friends. Part of me was still so sad about Daisy that I couldn't think about dating anyone. But another part of me was falling in love . . . with somebody else.

Laurel's world is about to change—forever. . . .

Find out how in
The Year I Turned Sixteen #3:
Laurel

THE YEAR

I TURNED

Sixteen

Four sisters. Four stories.

Calling All Sisters

National Sisters' Day is August 2nd!

Celebrate the bonds of sisterhood by telling us about your special relationship with your sister(s) and you could be published and pictured in *Girls' Life* magazine.

In fifty words or less, tell us about your relationship with your sister(s), and send along a photo. Winner gets her essay and photo published in *Girls' Life* magazine!

Send your Sisters' Day/*Girls' Life* essay and photo with your name, age, address, phone number, and parent's (or legal guardian's) signature saying it is okay to publish your entry and photo in *Girls' Life* to:

POCKET BOOKS: SISTERS' DAY/*GIRLS' LIFE* SWEEPSTAKES, 13TH FLOOR 1230 AVENUE OF THE AMERICAS, NEW YORK, NY 10020

Name _____ Age _____

Address_____

City _____State _____Zip Code _____

Phone Number (_____) _____

Parent's Signature _____

1494 (1of2)

Sisters' Day/*Girls' Life* Sweepstakes Official Rules

1. No purchase necessary. Enter by submitting your entry form and a typed or hand-printed essay that is no longer than 50 words and a photo of you and your sister(s). Please send them with your name, age, address, phone number, and parent's (or legal guardian's) signature saying it is okay to publish your entry and photo in *Girls' Life* to Pocket Books: Sisters' Day/Girls' Life Sweepstakes, 13th Floor, 1230 Avenue of the Americas, New York, NY 10020. Signed submissions constitute permission to publish entries in Girls' Life. Entries must be received by December 31, 1998. Not responsible for lost, late, damaged, stolen, illegible, mutilated, incomplete, postage-due, not delivered entries or for typographical errors in the entry form or rules. Entries are void if they are in whole or in part illegible, incomplete or damaged. You may enter as often as you wish, but each entry must be mailed separately. Winner will be selected at random from all eligible entries received in a drawing to be held on or about 1/7/99. Winner will be notified by mail.

2. Prize: essay and photo published in Girls' Life magazine (*approx. retail value: $500.00*). Prize not transferable and may not be substituted except by sponsor.

3. The sweepstakes is open to sisters ages 10-17 (as of June 9, 1998) who reside in the United States or Canada (excluding Quebec). Void in Puerto Rico and wherever prohibited or restricted by law. All federal, state and local laws apply. Employees and their families living in the same household, of Girls' Life and Viacom Inc., and their respective subsidiaries, affiliates, agencies, and participating retailers are not eligible.

4. The odds of winning depend upon the number of eligible entries received.

5. If a winner is a Canadian resident, then she must correctly answer a skill-based question administered by mail.

6. All expenses on receipt and use of prize including federal, state and local taxes are the sole responsibility of the winner. Winner's parent or legal guardian must execute and return an Affidavit of Eligibility and Liability/Publicity release within 15 days of notification attempt or an alternate winner will be selected.

7. Winner or winner's parents (or legal guardians) on winner's behalf grants to Pocket Books and Girls' Life the right to use her name and entry for any advertising, promotion, and publicity purposes without further compensation to or permission from the winner, except where prohibited by law, and the right to adapt, edit, and publish the winning entry.

8. By participating in this sweepstakes, entrants agree to be bound by these rules and the decision of the judges and sweepstakes sponsors, which are final in all matters relating to the sweepstakes.

9. The sweepstakes sponsors shall have no liability for any injury, loss or damage of any kind arising out of participation in this sweepstakes or the acceptance or use of the prize.

10. For the name of the prize winner (available after 1/15/99), send a stamped, self-addressed envelope to Prize Winner, Pocket Books: Sisters' Day/Girls' Life Sweepstakes, 13th Floor, 1230 Avenue of the Americas, New York, NY 10020.